ALSO BY DARCY COATES

The Haunting of Ashburn House
The Haunting of Blackwood House
The House Next Door
Craven Manor
The Haunting of Rookward House
The Carrow Haunt
Hunted
The Folcroft Ghosts
The Haunting of Gillespie House
Dead Lake
Parasite
Quarter to Midnight
Small Horrors

House of Shadows
House of Shadows
House of Secrets

THE HOUSE NEXT DOOR

DARCY COATES

Poisoned Pen
PRESS

Published by Poisoned Pen Press, an imprint of Sourcebooks
P.O. Box 4410, Naperville, Illinois 60567-4410
(630) 961-3900
sourcebooks.com

Originally self-published in 2017 by Black Owl Books.

Library of Congress Cataloging-in-Publication Data

Names: Coates, Darcy, author.
Title: House next door / Darcy Coates.
Description: Naperville, Illinois : Poisoned Pen Press, [2019] |
    Originally self-published in 2017 by Black Owl Books
Identifiers: LCCN 2019042394 | (trade paperback)
Subjects: GSAFD: Paranormal fiction.
Classification: LCC PR9619.4.C628 H68 2019 | DDC 823/.92--dc23
LC record available at https://lccn.loc.gov/2019042394

Printed and bound in the United States of America.
VP 10 9 8 7 6 5 4 3 2

CHAPTER 1

I LIVE NEXT TO a haunted house. It doesn't bother me too much. Most of the time, the Marwick residence is quiet—dormant— and nothing more than a two-story stack of old, lichen-coated stones, sash windows, and dying vines behind my fence.

The house is charming in its own way. It would have looked magnificent when it was new, before the porch's paint began to peel and the shingles fell askew. Still, even washing the cobweb-framed windows and reviving the long-dead garden would go a long way towards restoring its former dignity.

Most of my neighbours try to avoid the house. They don't look at it. They don't talk about it. Some actually cross the street when they need to pass it. I don't have that option. Only a thin picket fence divides my yard from Marwick's. I stare at its back twice a week when I hang out my laundry, and its front every morning when I water my garden.

I wouldn't say I've grown attached to it. But a fascination has slowly built over the four years I've lived beside the house. It's like an odd character at a formal dinner: I spend the first half of the night trying to avoid them, but by the end of the evening, I start to wonder if they might be the most interesting person there.

I don't know who built it or why, but the house looks nothing like the suburban homes surrounding it...and maybe that's a good thing.

I've known it's haunted for a while. My suspicions grew gradually, and before the twelfth of November, it was just little hints. My big tomcat likes to roam the neighbourhood and beg cuddles and treats off our neighbours. He'll dig up the garden of anyone who isn't friendly to him. He owns the entire street, but he never steps foot on the Marwick property.

Marwick's garden won't thrive, no matter how many new plants are dug in and watered dutifully. I've seen several families try. Their young shrubs and flowers wither and turn black after a few weeks. But two feet away, mine are flourishing.

I've seen three birds fly into its windows, apparently bent on self-destruction. I hear a bang, look up, and see a little ball of feathers tumble down the side of the house. It's heartbreaking. I can't explain why the birds choose to speed into the Marwick house when its windows are so dark and uninviting, but never fly into mine.

All of those things together grew into a steady wariness of the property. Or perhaps the wariness existed the day I moved in beside it, and that was what made me notice all of the small, strange occurrences. Either way, I didn't trust it. And following the evening of November twelfth, I knew I had good reason not to.

A woman's strangled scream woke me. I opened my eyes and rolled onto my back, staring at the ceiling, as my brain tried to come to terms with what had disturbed it.

The night was unpleasantly warm. I'd left my window open to invite in a non-existent breeze, and sweat stuck my pyjamas to my limbs. I pressed my thumbs into the corners of my eyes to wipe away the gunk that had collected there, then I rolled over to fall asleep again.

I blinked at the light pouring through my bedroom window. Someone was awake in the Marwick property. Maybe they'd stepped on one of their children's toys, or perhaps the mother had discovered the toilet seat left up one too many times. That could explain the scream.

But it didn't explain the gunshot.

I sat up, the crack echoing in my ears, and shuddered despite the heat. I hadn't just heard the gun fire, I'd seen the flash of white burst through the second-floor window. I wondered if they needed someone called. The police…an ambulance…it wouldn't be my first time phoning the emergency helpline over the Marwick property. They always took so long to respond, though. Far longer than for any other house in our street.

My toes dug into my bedroom carpet as I slid out of bed. I

crossed the room, drawn almost against my will, to watch the neighbouring house. Lights were turning on throughout the property. A woman wailed, her voice so high and strained that I couldn't understand the words. She was begging for something. I reached for my phone.

Another gunshot came from the room near the back of the house. I didn't know the family well, but they had three children, and I was fairly sure that the room belonged to their youngest son. Real, visceral fear woke me. I dialled the emergency helpline and held the phone up to my ear. I heard static in response.

More lights turned on, illuminating the house like a Christmas tree. A man ran past a window, his form a silhouette behind the curtains. He was carrying a child in one arm and a gun in the other. A woman followed closely. I could hear her words then. "Leave it…leave it, John. You can't hit it."

A child's cries rang through the stillness. The voice rose into a deafening shriek that drowned out the mother's. I followed the family's movements through the windows. They were going downstairs.

I redialled the emergency helpline as I mimicked the Marwick family's movements and descended my own stairs. Again, static. Had my phone broken? I was sure I'd remembered to pay the bill—

The Marwick's front door burst open. I stopped in my kitchen and bent across the bench to press my face against the window. I counted the shapes illuminated by the blocks of light escaping through the windows. Two large figures, three small. The whole family was there. Some of my fear eased, and I lowered the phone.

"In the car." The father put down the child in his arms and turned back to the house. He held his rifle close to his chest, using it as a shield more than a weapon. I could see the whites of his eyes flashing as he scanned his house.

As the mother pushed her children into the backseat, the youngest continued to wail. She didn't buckle them in. "John, come on."

He backed to the driver's side and reached behind himself to open the door, not taking his gaze off the house for even a moment. I watched him slink inside and heard the engine turn over. Tyres screamed on the driveway as the car pulled out then rocketed down the street, its trajectory so erratic that I was sure he was still watching the building over his shoulder.

Finally, the night fell quiet again. I leaned back from the kitchen window and dropped the phone to the bench. I wondered how many other neighbours had been woken by the screams and gunshots. Had any called the police? Were they pressed to their windows, like I was, watching with the same fascination drivers develop when passing a car accident?

If they were, none of them turned their lights on. The street remained dark and quiet. I waited in the kitchen for another few minutes then turned and climbed the stairs.

That was the last time I ever saw that family. I can't even remember their last name—to me, they were just "the Marwick family." That was the house's name, and it had been for as long as I'd lived in the street. They didn't return in the morning, as I'd expected, to collect their clothes. No one came for the furniture.

5

No one even turned out the lights. They stayed on for two full weeks until someone cancelled the contract and power to the house was cut. I hung blackout curtains over my windows for those two weeks and suffocated in the stifling heat of my improvised hotbox. On a few of those hot nights, I lay awake staring at my ceiling, completely naked and still overheated, and actually considered crossing over to the Marwick building, walking through the front door, which I knew had been left unlocked, and turning off the lights myself.

I never did. I was too afraid of what lived inside.

———

Following the night of November twelfth, the Marwick house stayed empty for eight months. It was the longest I'd ever seen it vacant. The building was peaceful during that time, like a giant who had fallen asleep on a hill and was gradually being coated in moss, until no one could tell it apart from the surrounding boulders. Some mornings, when I hung out my washing or watered the plants, I wouldn't even stare at the building's façade.

I asked around to see if any of my other neighbours knew why the last family had left. No one could tell me any more than what I'd seen with my own eyes; Faye Richmond, who lived on the house's other side, even seemed surprised when I told her the building was empty. Eventually, I stopped thinking about it, and the memory began to seem less dramatic and less exciting as time wore away at it.

I'd passed the For Sale sign so often that it looked unnatural when Sold was eventually plastered over it. It was like an old friend growing a moustache; there was nothing *wrong* with it, but the change was still uncomfortable.

Barely four days after the sign changed to Sold, it was taken down, and that same afternoon, a small rental truck pulled into the driveway.

I'm a curious person. I don't feel ashamed to admit it. Curiosity does a lot of good; from what I gathered, no one else tried to call the emergency helpline on the night the previous family fled. Curiosity has led me to find abandoned kittens in drains and to notice when Mr. Parker didn't leave for work one Wednesday morning. He'd had a stroke in the night. Curiosity saved him from lying on his kitchen floor until he starved. So I don't feel embarrassed to say I was curious about the new family.

I'd already watered my plants that morning, but even though it was overcast, I decided the day was warm enough to warrant a second dose. I sidled along the fence, watering can pouring liquid onto the still-wet ground, and peeked at my new neighbour. She surprised me. I'd been expecting a family—the building was big enough to house at least three children and maybe grandparents, as well—but she seemed to be alone. She was young and small, and her mousy brown-blonde hair was pulled into a ponytail.

She's awfully small to be living in the Marwick house. My watering can was empty, but I kept miming the tipping motion. *And to be living there alone, too.*

I don't know why it unsettled me as much as it did. Maybe it was because I wouldn't have felt safe living there alone, and she seemed so much more vulnerable than I was. Maybe it was the feeling that she would need an ally, but so clearly didn't have one. She unloaded the truck herself. It didn't contain much.

One of my cats, Dusty, had wandered out to see what I was doing. I scratched under her chin. "Whatcha think, Dust? Should I pay her a visit?"

Dusty gave my wrist a love bite then frisked into the bushes, probably to hunt for lizards or insects she could eat. I looked back at the Marwick house. The lights were coming on again for the first time in eight months.

I'd never actually seen inside, except to peek through the windows. Was the Marwick's interior just as grim as the outside? I scanned the chipped grey stone front, its lichen and vines the only plants that seemed to survive, then set my watering can down.

Like I said, I'm a curious person. Sometimes that's a good thing.

CHAPTER 2

I HURRIEDLY PREPARED A batch of muffins. Cooking is my hobby, and I always have some kind of baked goods lying around the place, but I felt like a new neighbour deserved something fresh. Muffins were by far the fastest and easiest gift to cook. Combine sugar, flour, eggs, and milk, then mix through whatever sweet things are available. For that batch, it was bananas, so ripe they were threatening to spoil. Fifteen minutes in the oven, and the muffins were ready.

Those fifteen minutes were some of the longest I've ever sat through. I wiped down my bench twice, fiddled with the kitchen's curtains to give me a better view of the Marwick house, and fished a basket and tea towel out of the cupboards. Then I bent low and stared at the rising batter as though I could make the muffins cook faster through sheer force of will.

As soon as they looked close enough to done, I pulled them

out and threw them into the basket, earning a couple of burnt fingers for my impatience. I met Bell in the hallway. She carried a live lizard in her jaws but dashed towards the living room before I could stop her. There was no time to chase her. I resigned myself to having a lizard living in my home.

Our street has generous gardens for a suburban area. It takes me fifteen paces to reach my front gate, then another twelve to follow the footpath to the Marwick's, and a further fifteen to her front porch. The porch had been painted white at one point, but the grey wood showed through clearly. Fissures ran up the grains, and the boards groaned, making me feel as if it were about to collapse out from under me.

The front door stood open, but I stopped on the mat and knocked. I caught a quick glance of dark wood, long red curtains, and a twisting staircase before my new neighbour appeared in the doorway to block my view, looking shocked and frazzled. Her hair was coming out of its ponytail, and her T-shirt had slipped askew. My first impression was of large, round eyes, like a deer shocked by the apparition of some predator. She stared at me, her mouth open a fraction, then said, "Sorry, I wasn't expecting you."

"No. You shouldn't have. I mean, you didn't have any reason to." I'd never been good at meeting people. Has there ever been such a bad combination as chronic curiosity and social awkwardness? I thrust the basket out ahead of myself, hoping an offering of food would soften my abrupt greeting. "Muffins. For you. I'm your neighbour."

"Oh. Oh!" The wariness broke into a smile. I couldn't be sure if it was my imagination running away or not, but she actually looked relieved. "Wow, thank you. Um, I'm Anna. Did you want to come in?"

"Yes. Josephine. Jo. That's me. Yes." *Stop talking. You sound like an idiot.*

Anna laughed and stepped back. "All right, but I have to warn you, this place is still a mess. It came furnished, but everything's covered in dust. You would have thought the old owners would pay for a cleaner or something, huh?"

"Yeah." I didn't tell her about the terror I'd seen on the old owners' faces. "Are you living here alone?"

She hesitated. "At the moment, yes."

We passed through the foyer. It really was like something out of a mansion. A runner matching the blood-red carpet curled up the length of the staircase leading to the second floor. The windows were all framed with heavy matching red curtains. There wasn't much furniture, but what existed was understated but classical.

"Through here…I think." Anna turned a corner. "Oh, good, it *is* the kitchen. I'm still getting used to this place."

I laughed, but I couldn't stop staring at the house's interior. What I'd seen of the previous family had made me think they were fairly normal. The children had worn T-shirts, ridden bikes, and screamed with laughter. The mother had smoked, and the father had worked some kind of construction job. But the house looked nothing like a normal suburban family home. It dripped with importance, every part of it stately, reserved, and aged. Anna turned to face me in the kitchen's entryway, and it struck me that she looked dwarfed by the house. Like a tiny morsel lying on its tongue, waiting to be swallowed.

Maybe I was just hungry.

"I brought muffins." I was repeating myself, but I didn't know what else to say. "Banana."

"They smell really good. I forgot to have breakfast this morning. Can I get you some, uh…tea? I think I have tea." She began opening cupboards and drawers. "Oh, looks like they left coffee, too. That was considerate."

Eight-month-old coffee would be well past stale. "Tea's good. Here, I can help."

I put the basket on the centre of the wooden table and helped Anna sort through her drawers. I washed two cups and plates while she boiled the kettle then chose one of the herbal teas she'd found in a drawer.

It felt strangely wrong to be using the whitegoods and tea left by the previous owners, almost like trespassing, as if they would be scandalised to know what was happening in their home.

They left it here, I reminded myself as I threw out the teabag. *They didn't want it anymore.*

If I had to guess, Anna felt the same. She flitted around the kitchen, seemingly reluctant to touch most of the things in the cupboard.

"It will feel more like home once you've been living here a while," I said.

She gave me a quick smile and dusted her hands on her jeans

as she took a seat at the table. "Yeah, I guess it will. It's just surreal. It all happened so fast."

"What made you move?" I passed her a muffin, which she took gratefully and cut into cubes.

"Oh, just life being unpredictable. There were some problems with my old house. I couldn't stay there any longer."

There are some problems with this house, too. I didn't have much experience welcoming neighbours, but I was pretty sure telling them their house was haunted was the sort of thing people weren't supposed to do.

But at the same time, it seemed unfair not to tell her about something so major. I struggled to find a middle ground. "This place has been empty for a while."

"Has it?" She looked around the kitchen, taking in the dark-wood cabinets and granite benches. "It was a bargain. Surprising no one else wanted it."

"Yeah." I watched her closely. She didn't *look* surprised. I had a suspicion she knew why the Marwick property had been untenanted for so long, and we were just dancing around the subject. I pushed a little harder. "This place has a bit of a reputation."

She shot me a glance. Her eyes were bright blue; I hadn't noticed before. Then I realised she hadn't made eye contact before. Her voice dropped very low. "The real estate agent hinted at that. She said some families have had trouble living here. Some…unexplained stuff."

"Ghosts." It felt good to say the word and not get stared at like I was crazy. "Do you…believe in ghosts?"

She ran a hand over her mouth then blew out a breath and laughed. "That's a heavy question, huh? I've never seen one. But I'm open-minded. I think there's more to this world than we can see." She sent another very quick peek towards me. "What about you?"

I shrugged. "I never gave it much thought until moving here." *But yes, I believe in them now.*

We didn't speak for a moment. Anna stared at her teacup, her muffin only half eaten, then said, "How much do you know about this house? Is it really bad?"

I suddenly felt guilty. I'd meant to warn her, not frighten her. "No, I mean, it's not…uh…"

My words died into a mumble, and Anna's brows pulled together. I couldn't in good conscience tell her everything was fine. But I didn't want her lying awake at night, terrified, either. I collected myself and licked my lips. "I don't know much about it, sorry. But it's not like what you see in the movies. There's some weird stuff that happens. But they're pretty minor. My cats avoid it. And, uh…" *It would be unkind not to tell her.* "The last family left in a rush in the middle of the night. But I've never actually seen a ghost in the house or anything. No one's been hurt. That I know of."

"Okay." She picked her cup up and took a sip. "I can handle that."

I narrowed my eyes as I watched her. She looked anxious but, at the same time, strangely resigned.

The next question fell out of me before I could stop it. "If you knew this place had a reputation, why did you move here?"

"I needed somewhere to stay but was short on both time and money." She seemed to be choosing her words carefully. "This place was really, really cheap. Way cheaper than it should have been for its size. I knew that meant there was something wrong with it. But I could afford it, and they let me move in quickly. Sometimes you need to make sacrifices for good things."

"Oh." There seemed to be a lot she wasn't telling me, but I didn't want to make her uncomfortable by pushing further. I looked over my shoulder, through the doorway leading into a living room. The lighting was muted, and like the rest of the furniture, the chairs were large and stately. "It's a really nice house. If the reputation doesn't bother you, it's an absolute steal."

"Yeah?" She brightened a fraction. "It's nice to have a place to call my own. And all of this old furniture must be worth a fortune. The agent said it comes from when the house was first furnished."

"Really?" *Ah, I didn't think it looked like the last family's style.*

"And there's plenty of space for a home office. At my old place, I had to work on this little corner table in my bedroom." She laughed. "Paint got over everything. It was a nightmare."

"You work from home? What do you do?"

"I repurpose dolls. Barbies, Bratz, character miniatures, or any plastic figurine that needs a makeover." She nodded towards the foyer. "Want to see? I have a couple in a box back there."

"All right." I followed her back to the main room. We seemed to have found a subject she enjoyed, because she chatted freely as she opened and sifted through the box.

"All of these mass-market plastic dolls come off the production line looking so soulless. I buy them from op-shops, or sometimes even find them thrown out, and fix them up. I repaint their faces, sometime cut or re-weave their hair, and give them new outfits. Like this one."

She pressed a doll into my hands. I guessed it would have once been a Bratz, but it was unrecognisable. Instead of the garish makeup and pouty oversized lips, it wore a warm smile. Anna had painted over its eyes to make them proportionate to the other features and had even given it freckles. It looked sweet—like a country farm girl, an impression heightened by the tiny denim overalls.

"This is really nice." I didn't have to fake my surprise.

"Thanks." She bounced on the balls of her feet, apparently too full of excitement and joy to keep still. "Parents love them, especially in the home-schooling and alternative communities. They appreciate having a one-of-a-kind doll, and the fact that they're recycled doesn't hurt, either."

"Yeah, I can imagine that. Do you sell them at fetes?"

"Online, mostly." Anna took the doll back and tucked it into the box. "I upload new batches every few weeks. They sell really fast. I'm hoping I'll be able to spend more time making them now that…well, now that I have this house." The joy that had lit her face softened.

I hunted for something to bring it back. "I'm sure you will. Have you picked a workroom yet?"

"No, not yet. I thought maybe one of the upstairs ones. I

like having a view. But I haven't been up there since the agent whisked me through." Anna glanced towards the staircase then turned a sheepish smile on me. "Did you want to…have a look with me?"

CHAPTER 3

THE CURVING STAIRCASE GROANED as we crept up to the second floor. Part of me felt guilty for enjoying myself so much. The other part was just excited to finally explore inside Marwick House.

Watercolour paintings hung on the walls, alternately depicting nature scenes and small animals. The animals were all slightly wrong; the eyes weren't level, one ear seemed larger than the other, or its pose was contorted. I wondered if those paintings were part of the original furnishings, too. Had each of the house's occupants walked in to the same surroundings then walked out, leaving it virtually untouched for the next family?

Anna stopped at the top of the stairs. The hallway was poorly lit, and the light refracted from the lower floor painted her face with odd shadows. She stared down the hall. "It doesn't look this large from the outside."

"No," I agreed.

She took a hesitant step down the hall. I moved up to her side to offer what reassurance I could.

"It's strange with furniture in it." She laughed, but there wasn't much strength behind it. "I know that must sound odd—houses are supposed to be furnished—but these beds and desks and wardrobes aren't mine, and that makes me feel like I don't belong here."

It was the same sensation I'd felt earlier, while eating off the previous family's dishes, as if we were intruders taking advantage of their property while they were on holiday.

"It's your house," I said, putting conviction behind the words. "It belongs to you. No one else."

The door at the end of the hall groaned as it shifted closed.

Both Anna and I jumped. I laughed and patted her shoulder. "Someone must have left the window open."

"Yeah. Probably." She tried to match my chuckles but stayed rooted to the spot.

We both watched the door. It didn't move.

"Come on." I led the way. "One of the rooms has got to be a good place to work. Do you need any sort of special arrangement to make your dolls?"

"N-No." She glanced through each partially open door we passed. Most were bedrooms. "Just desk space and—and good lighting."

The upstairs floor was all wood panelling. I ran my fingers over the planks, feeling their little grooves and bumps. A splinter

19

caught on my index finger, and I pulled it back with a murmur. *Should've been more careful.*

"Jo?" Anna's voice was a whisper. She tugged on my jacket. "Did you see that?"

"See what?" I followed her gaze towards the room at the end of the hall, the one with the shifting door. It was open just a sliver, revealing blue wallpaper and a hint of natural light. I squinted and took a step closer. A woman paced through the room.

I took a quick, sharp breath. She'd been visible for only a fraction of a second. I'd caught a glimpse of a washed-out slate-blue dress and sallow, shadowed eyes. Then she was gone again.

When I tried to step back, I bumped into Anna. Her voice was ragged with stress. "You saw her, too, didn't you?"

Has someone been staying in the house? I didn't want to move, but I forced my legs to carry me closer to the room. I stretched out a hand and bumped the door. The hinges wailed as the door glided open. Inside was empty.

"No one." The anxious squeeze didn't leave my chest. I couldn't figure out if an empty room was better or worse than finding a squatter. Anna came up beside me. She crouched to peer under the wooden desk then stood and released a breath in a rush.

"Oh! Look! It was just the curtain."

The windows had been left open. The heavy drapes framing them billowed out in a gust of wind. They were the right shade of slate blue to be confused for a woman's dress and in the right position to be visible through the door's gap, but as I stared at them, I found myself less willing to be convinced than Anna. The curtains had no eyes.

Anna's mood had lifted again, though. She chuckled as she stepped into the room and admired its furniture and blue wallpaper. The space was larger than the bedrooms but sparsely fitted, and the window looked over the rooftops at the treed hills in the distance. "This is a really nice space." She traced a finger over the desk's surface. "Lots of natural light. Maybe this could be my workroom."

"Maybe." The walls were too dark and the rug too badly worn for me to like the space. I didn't want to influence her choice by letting reluctance into my voice, but it slipped in regardless. "Let's have a look at what else this house has."

Anna nodded and followed me back to the hallway. We stepped into each room we passed. Some clearly hadn't been lived in for some time. Others showed signs of recent inhabitation. Clothes hung in the wardrobes of the children's rooms, where toys were scattered over the floor.

"The last family really did leave in a rush, huh?" Anna stopped in one of the boys' rooms. The bed sheets lay in a pool on the floor. She rubbed at her arms. "I'm surprised they didn't come back for anything. The furniture's one thing, but wouldn't you get your clothes?"

I could see the side of my own house through the window. It might have been the room I'd seen the flash of gunfire in. My eyes drifted over the wood panelling until they landed on a small black hole in the wall, near the window. *I bet if we dug into the wood, we'd find the bullet there.*

"Jo?"

"Yeah?"

"How long did the last family live here?"

"Not long." I scoured my memory. "Three months. Maybe three and a half. The family before that was a year. The one before that cancelled and left during the buyer's remorse period. The one before that was here when I arrived."

"Okay." She brushed some of her fine hair away from her face. "That's a quick turnover."

"Yeah, I guess it is." I tried to think of something to make it seem a little less grim. "They probably didn't like the neighbourhood. There are lots of older people around here. Hardly any kids. And no convenient public transport. It's no wonder they didn't want to stay, huh?"

"Maybe." She gave me a small smile and kicked at the discarded sheets. "Either way, the house was cheap. I can put up with some quirks for that."

When we returned to the foyer, I was surprised by a taste of fresh air coming through the open door. I'd gotten used to the house's stuffy, dusty atmosphere. Through one of the doorways, I caught a glimpse of a grand piano. I wasn't surprised; the building felt like it needed a dignified instrument to round out the atmosphere.

Anna stared at the unpacked boxes for a moment, and I wondered what she was thinking. Was she trying to imagine where she would find room for her own life amongst a stranger's house? Or was she afraid of unpacking, knowing that it would be a commitment to stay, and that she would risk leaving her own possessions behind if she had to flee during the night?

"Jo?" She folded her arms over her chest. Her posture belied that she was nervous, but at least now she looked me in the eyes. "Can I ask a favour?"

"Yeah, sure."

"On my website, could I list your address instead of mine?" She must have seen the confusion on my face, because she quickly added, "Probably no one will visit. I just have to have a public address there by law. But...I'd rather not use my real address. I want to try to separate myself from my old life as much as possible. If that makes sense."

It didn't, but I shrugged. "Sure. I don't mind."

"Thank you." Some of the tightness around her eyes relaxed. "And, um, if anyone ever does ask after me, could you...pretend like you don't know me?"

Ah. So you're hiding from someone. The rush into purchasing the house suddenly made more sense. "Yeah, of course. As far as strangers are concerned, I don't know a single Anna."

She grinned. "Thanks. I owe you one."

Sunlight came through the window at a sharp angle. I'd spent more time in Marwick House than I'd expected and suddenly felt bad for taking up so much of Anna's day. I waved towards the door. "I'd better head home, anyway. Thanks for letting me have a look around. And good luck with the dolls."

"Oh, your basket—"

"Keep it. I've got plenty more." I stepped through the door, and Anna followed to lean on the frame.

"Are you sure?"

"Yeah, absolutely."

"Thanks for coming over. I'm glad we're neighbours."

"Me, too." It wasn't until I was halfway down the driveway that I realised how much I'd meant it. Somehow, between hunting for clean cups and being scared by the drifting curtain, we'd become friends. I wanted to see more of Anna…and her house.

Stepping into my own overgrown garden was like teleporting into another world. Duke, my roaming tom, ran across the street when he saw me. He followed me inside, where I shed my jacket at the door and flexed my shoulders. Duke moseyed around my feet, smelling my shoes, then clamped his ears onto his head and backed away.

"What?" I laughed at his expression. "Do my feet smell or something?"

He huffed out a breath and disappeared up the stairs, probably to claim his spot on the end of my bed. I continued into the kitchen to put the kettle on, and I found Bell, my third cat, sitting on her window-view cat climber. She was in a crouch, her eyes fixed on Marwick House, the fur along her spine poked up in a ridge. As I neared, I caught a low, frightened rumble reverberating from her throat.

"Not you, too." I scratched behind her ears, but she wouldn't even look at me.

CHAPTER 4

I DIDN'T SEE MUCH of Anna during the following days. Sometimes, we passed each other in the garden and called out a greeting, and sometimes, I glimpsed her through the windows. She would wave to me and always smiled broadly. She looked happy. I was glad; the first night after she'd moved in, I'd sat up until after midnight just in case she had any problems, but her lights had stayed off, and the house had remained quiet. She seemed to be settling into Marwick without issue.

Even so, a lingering shroud of unease clung to me. Maybe it was because another bird had flown into the Marwick house's windows the day after Anna moved in. I'd peered over the fence to see if it was all right, but it lay on its back on the stones below the window, its head twisted unnaturally far back.

My cats remained wary, too. Duke spent more time indoors than usual and gave the Marwick house a wide berth whenever he passed it. Dusty and Bell alternated perches by the windows and watched the house. Occasionally, they growled at nothing.

Watching the others in the street, I noticed something strange. None of my other neighbours visited Anna—at least, none that I saw. But one by one, they closed the curtains on the windows facing the Marwick house. I wondered if it was a conscious choice or just a subconscious response to the same niggling unease that had dogged me since the house became occupied. Or perhaps my imagination was getting out of control. The temperature was growing colder as autumn changed to winter. People would be closing their curtains to keep the heat inside their houses.

Four days after Anna moved in, I was shaken out of the novel I was reading by a knock at the door. I rarely had visitors. What I'd told Anna about the street was true; almost all of our neighbours were elderly and often cranky, as well. Anna had to be a few years younger than I was. I jumped out of my chair and jogged to the door, wondering if Anna had come for a casual visit or if she'd perhaps seen something unusual in her new house.

A tall, thin man stood on my porch, his hands thrust into his jacket's pockets. He smiled when I opened the door. It wasn't an expression of happiness, just a perfunctory flattening and widening of his lips to push out his cheeks.

"Hey, Lukas." I sighed. "What do you want?"

"Hey, Grumpy," he retorted. "Move, I'm coming in."

He didn't ask if it was a good time for a visit. We both knew I had nothing better to do. I shifted aside so he could fit down my hallway.

"Coffee," he said as he threw his jacket over the back of a kitchen chair. "In one of the cups the cats don't use."

I pulled a face at him. I almost never let the cats drink out of my own cups. They couldn't fit their faces inside very well, anyway. "What do you want?" I repeated as I put the kettle on and set out two cups. Out of spite, I deliberately gave him one Duke used.

"Mum wanted me to make sure you hadn't died." Lukas picked dirt out from under his fingernail. "She's got this complex that you're going to pass away one day and your cats will have eaten your face off before anyone finds you."

"It's none of Aunt Bea's business when I die or how much I'm consumed," I said. "Please kindly ask her to keep her nose in her own business."

"You're cranky today."

I slammed the milk carton onto the bench. "I wasn't until you showed up. I know why she sent you. She wants you to act like her spy so that she can gloat about how her own family is so much better than mine. If she really cared, she'd come herself."

"Ouch." His lip curled. "You really *are* mad. For what it's worth, Mum does actually care about you. Not that it matters"—he returned to picking at his fingernail—"but I think she doesn't visit because she feels guilty."

Wanting the conversation to end, I focussed on making Lukas's coffee.

"Oh, and she wants me to bring back some of your brownies. The ones with crack cocaine in them."

"I don't put drugs in my cooking," I grumbled.

"But then why do they taste so good?"

I snorted. I couldn't stay mad at him, no matter how hard I tried. Lukas gave me a grin, a proper one—big, wolfish, and too wide for his face. I pushed his mug across the bench to him. "All right, flatterer, you'll get your brownies. But you'll have to pay me in gossip. What news of the outside world?"

"Millie's netball team won the season. Her coach says she has a good chance of being scouted next year. But personally, I suspect he's just saying that to keep us paying for his lessons."

I hadn't seen Millie, Lukas's younger sister, in years. The last time I'd been in my aunt's house, Millie had been eight and obsessed with horses. "She must be excited."

"She is. She thinks she's going to play in the Olympics." He took a sip of his coffee. "Hm. Harsh and bitter. Just like me."

With a snicker, I began lining brownie ingredients up on the bench. "What's up with your life? How's that new partnership thing working out? You were really excited about it last time you visited."

He grimaced. "Ah, yes, the flaming *Titanic* of deals. So much promise. So much suffering. I keep forgetting you haven't heard yet."

My heart sank. Lukas was an amateur film director. He was actually good, and it wasn't just family loyalty making me say that; two of his films had been well-received at Sundance, and he'd recently become a partner at a small but promising film company. "Oh boy. What happened?"

"You remember me telling you about Joel, my new business

partner? I remember raving about how talented he was and how he had all of these amazing connections." Lukas rubbed a hand over his face. "Damn, I was an idiot. Well, that very same Joel stole our start-up money and fled overseas."

"What?" I dropped a cupful of flour into the bowl. "He can't do that."

Lukas pursed his lips and spread his hands. "You'd think that. But apparently, stealing from your partners is a well-respected tradition in the business industry."

"No, but I mean, you had a contract, right? I know you would. You're too cynical about everyone and everything to do business without one."

"Yeah, we had a great contract. Watertight. I ran it past a lawyer and everything." Lukas folded his hands on the bench and flopped forward to rest his head on them. His voice was muffled, but I could still hear him clearly. "That contract would do amazing things if there was any way to get him to court. He pulled our money out of our account one Friday night, hopped on a jet, and, as far as I can tell, is residing somewhere in India. It would be a nightmare to extradite him…and even that would only be possible if we could actually *find* him."

"Oh. Lukas. I'm sorry." I felt ghastly. He'd put all of his savings—including the awards he'd won for his films and the money he'd earned from selling DVDs privately—into the business. That deal was meant to be his big break.

"Don't be." Lukas finally lifted his head. His smile was equal parts resigned and bitter. "As my girlfriend said, it's just the fee for a valuable life lesson. She left me, by the way. Apparently, the tattoo artist was sticking more than needles into her, and she rather liked it."

I didn't know what to say, except, "Dude, your life sucks."

"Thank you, Jo. It's a great comfort to hear that."

"I'm going to put extra chocolate chips in your brownies."

"Now that *is* welcome news." When he reached over to dip his finger into the batter, I didn't even try to stop him.

"I've got something to tell you, anyway," I said. "It won't cheer you up, but maybe it will distract you from your fugue of suffering for a few minutes."

"Distract away."

"A new lady moved into the house next door." I told him about Anna, how we'd explored the house, and seeing what we'd thought was a woman behind the door. His face remained passively sceptical through the entire story, but I didn't let that bother me. Passively sceptical was his default setting.

At the end of my story, he said, "That's it?"

"So far. She's only been there for four days." I narrowed my eyes at him. "You don't think it's haunted."

"I think it's a very intriguing but ultimately unremarkable building." He went back for another taste of the batter. "And that living with eighteen cats has sent you slightly insane."

"Three cats. *Three.*" I set to greasing and lining a pan. "But I swear there's something weird about that house. Anna's lovely, though. Kinda young to be living alone, but she runs her own business and seems sensible enough."

"Hmm." He longingly watched me empty the mixing bowl and throw it into the sink.

"Hey, I have an idea. You could set up your cameras in the house and record what happens there. It could be like a documentary."

"Thank you for the offer, but I think I've ruined my professional reputation enough for one lifetime."

"You're the worst."

"And proud of it."

I pulled up a seat opposite while we waited for the brownies to cook. Lukas updated me on everything that was happening on his side of the family. It had been several months since his last visit, and there was a lot to hear. As the stories stacked on top of each other, their weight depressed me. Every one of our relatives had at least three or four significant events happening in their lives; all I had to tell him about was a haunted house. I didn't even have a job I could complain about. It made me feel empty and lonely. Maybe Aunt Bea had good reason to worry about cats eating my face.

The brownies came out of the oven, and I sliced them as soon as they were cool enough. As was our habit, Lukas offered to pay for them. I vehemently refused. I knew I'd find a twenty-dollar note hidden somewhere in the garden or the hallway after he'd left. As much as I wanted to make the brownies a gift, he seemed incapable of accepting them as such.

As we meandered towards the front door, a knock interrupted our conversation. Lukas and I looked at each other, and I suspect we were thinking the same thing: how many stars had aligned for Jo to get *two* visitors in a single day?

I opened the door. Anna waited outside, her hands knit together and her face tense. She twitched when she saw Lukas. "I'm so sorry. You have company. I didn't mean to interrupt—"

"Just leaving," Lukas said brusquely. He sidestepped both of us and waved over his shoulder as he sauntered towards his car. "See you in another few months, Jo. Try to die somewhere the cats can't reach you."

CHAPTER 5

"SORRY. THAT WAS JUST my cousin." I smiled at Anna. She seemed to be trying to edge back towards her own house, so I beckoned to her before she could lose whatever courage had carried her to my door. "Come on in. The kettle's still warm."

"Only if I'm not intruding."

"Of course not! I love company. And you're way more welcome than grumpy-face Lukas."

Anna finally smiled and slipped inside after me. I regretted not saving any of the brownies, but I still had spiced fruitcake from the previous day that I pulled out of the cupboard.

"Make yourself at home. And, uh, sorry about the cats. They get curious about strangers."

As if on cue, my three cats drifted in from different parts of the house to sniff at Anna's legs. She laughed and patted them.

"They're gorgeous. I knew the big grey cat was yours, but I didn't know you had more."

"Yeah, I'm the street's crazy cat lady. Dusty and Bell don't like going outside. Dusty gets brambles in her fur, and Bell is just lazy."

Duke flattened his ears to his head and backed away from Anna. I wondered what he smelt that he didn't like.

Anna carefully took a seat at the kitchen counter. She accepted the cup I passed her. "Oh, I almost forgot! I made you a present." She fished inside her bag then handed me a loose parcel of crepe paper. I unwrapped it and found a small doll, its repainted face smiling up at me. The long brown hair had been given a fringe and plaited. Anna had dressed it in a cute blue-checked dress and a cardigan with an oversized button. "Wow! You made it for me?"

"Yeah." Her smile was small but excited. "I put a lot of care into it. I mean, I put care into all of my dolls, but this one especially—"

"Thank you. I love it." I set the doll on the windowsill and arranged it carefully so that it sat upright. "Does it have a name?"

"That's up to you."

"Oh, no. I'm awful at names. I named my cat Tinkerbell because she had a collar with a jingly bell." I laughed. "I took the collar off once she decided to be an indoors-only cat, so now the name doesn't even make sense."

"I think it's a cute name." Anna blew on her drink. I sat opposite, and for a minute, neither of us seemed to know what to say.

"Is everything going well with the new house?" I asked.

"Oh, yeah, I mean, it's been good. A lot of work. I cleared out the clothes and toys from the last family. I just didn't feel comfortable with them there—like it was still their house." She brushed her long hair behind her ear. "I tried to find their contact details to see if they wanted any of it back, but the agent had lost touch with them, so I donated what I could and threw out the rest."

"Is it helping the house feel more like yours?"

"I bit, I think." She shrugged. "I'm still getting used to it. And still getting lost, can you believe? Whoever designed the building's floor plan must have been insane. Rooms open into other rooms you wouldn't expect, and the hallway does this weird loopy thing that disorients me."

"I hope you at least decided on a workroom."

"Oh, yes, I did! That lovely blue room at the end of the hallway, the one that frightened us. Remember?"

I wouldn't forget that place in a hurry. "Yeah. Glad you're getting settled."

We lapsed into another silence, which lasted almost uncomfortably long. Anna stared at her tea. Her face had lost its earlier brightness, and I guessed there was something she wanted to tell me but couldn't bring herself to say.

I leaned forward and lowered my voice. "Is something wrong?"

She startled then gave a hesitant smile. "No. I mean…no. I've just been a bit rattled; that's all. You know, new house, new neighbourhood, and you're the only person here I know. I tried to say hello to my neighbour on the other side when she was watering her lawn yesterday, but she just glared at me and went back inside."

"Oh, Mrs. Richmond. Sorry about her. She's awful. Constantly grouchy and tries to hose Duke when he wanders into her yard."

"At least it's not just me, then." She chewed on her lip. "A bird flew into the window."

"The sparrow a few days ago? They do that sometimes."

"No. I found the sparrow and threw it out. This was an owl last night. It hit the window while I was painting a doll. Scared me so badly, I ruined the face and had to redo it."

"That's sad. I love owls."

"Me, too. It's a big one. I'm surprised the glass didn't shatter." She looked down at her cup. "It's such a beautiful bird it, feels wrong to throw it in the bin. I was thinking of burying it."

"Hey, that's a good idea." I looked at Marwick House through the kitchen window. "Did you want company? I don't have plans for today."

"Yes! Yes, please."

I'd found Anna's real motive for visiting. She was afraid and lonely and didn't want to carry out a funeral service on her own.

I washed up the cups, then we collected our jackets and followed the circuitous route from my garden to hers. Once again, I was struck by just how different her property's atmosphere was. I could almost feel the temperature drop.

"It's just around here." Anna led me down the side of her house. Vines grew between the stones of the path, taking up the spaces where even grass refused to thrive, and their brittle stems crackled under my shoes. We found the owl crumpled at the side of the house, one wing thrown out, its head tilted back. I didn't know birds well, but I thought it might be a young barn owl. I looked up. A smear of white powder marked the second-floor window. "You're right. It's lucky it didn't break through the glass."

"Poor thing," Anna said. "This never happened at my old house."

I didn't especially want to touch it, but I knew Anna didn't, either, so I gingerly picked the owl up by its leg. The creature was stiff with rigor mortis, but clumps of feathers came away as I moved it. "Where did you want to bury it?"

"Uh…" Anna scanned the yard. Only a handful of plants grew there, and they were all lopsided or gnarled. "What about by the big tree up the back?"

"Perfect." I held the dead owl at arm's length as I carried it towards its resting place. A small shed was nestled in the yard's corner, so I placed the owl on the dirt beside the tree and went in search of a shovel. The shed was locked with a rusty padlock. With Anna's permission, I found a hefty rock and bashed it against the lock, which came off on the third try.

Inside smelt mildewy and musty. Long-dormant cobwebs crusted the benches and shelves, and the windows were so dirty that very little natural light got through. It was clear none of the recent families had spent much time in the shed. I found a shovel and used my sleeve to knock the cobwebs off before picking it up.

"Here?" I asked, digging the shovel's tip into the dirt below the tree. Anna nodded, so I applied my boot and dug out a chunk of earth. I flipped it aside and went back for more. I didn't know how deep an owl's grave should be, so I decided to just dig as far as I could.

"Jo." Anna's voice was soft and filled with confused wonder.

I tipped another shovel of dirt aside and looked back at her. "What's up?"

"There are bones. Look."

I turned to the freshly dug soil, where off-white lumps were mixed with the brown earth. Horrified, I used the shovel's blade to knock some of them free.

We'd accidentally dug up a grave. The tiny skull looked as though it belonged to a rat. But there were other bones that must have come from larger animals, too: cats, possibly even dogs. I looked back at my hole. More white protrusions poked out of the earth.

"There are so many," I muttered. This wasn't a grave for a single, loved animal. It was a mass burial.

Anna's cheeks had blanched white. She rubbed her hands over the back of her neck, looking nauseous. "Why? Why would… who would…"

"Hey, it's all right." I wished my voice would carry the reassurance I tried to project into it. "This is a nice corner of the garden. It's not surprising other people decided to bury their pets here."

Anna shuddered. "This was a bad idea. We shouldn't have dug it up. Bad idea."

"No, hey, it's fine." I picked up the owl and dropped it into the hole. It landed on the white-flecked dirt with a thud. "It's fine. We'll bury them all back. It's fine."

I scooped shovelfuls of dirt over the owl as Anna hung back, arms wrapped around her torso and her blue eyes wide. She didn't move or look away until all of the soil was back in the hole—raised into a small mound, thanks to the owl's bulk—and I'd patted the surface over.

"I'm sorry," she said at last. "I shouldn't have asked you to do that."

"It's fine." That was going to be my new mantra if I wasn't careful. Anxiety had made my skin pucker into goose bumps, and a trickle of cold sweat ran down between my shoulder blades. I resolutely kept my smile in place. "Not a problem. All dealt with."

We both stared at the lump of dark, freshly turned soil. I didn't like any of the questions it presented: not the *who*, and especially not the *why*. What I'd said earlier was true—it was a nice corner, under the tree. Probably the nicest part of the yard. But from what I'd seen, there were at least a dozen animals buried there... and no hints on how much deeper the hole went.

CHAPTER 6

IN THE DAYS AFTER the funeral, I saw little of Anna. Twice, we waved to each other when we passed in the gardens, and I sometimes saw her walking to and from the corner shops three blocks away. Otherwise, Marwick was silent. Anna was either avoiding me or consumed by her work. I didn't mind either way.

The bones had rattled me more than I wanted to admit. When I worked in my back garden or hung out washing, my gaze drifted over the fence towards the clump of dirt under the tree. I was grateful that Anna wasn't pursuing the friendship. And that, in turn, made me feel guilty. Anna was alone; based on the complete absence of visitors, she was even lonelier than I was. It wasn't fair to avoid her for something she had no control over.

But the house no longer fascinated me. Very slowly, my curiosity was turning to repulsion. There was something wrong with the building. The shadows were too thick. The vines coiling up its walls as though trying to strangle the stones seemed too dark and twisted to be real plants.

Sometimes, lights turned on in the middle of the night and stayed on until dawn. I told myself that it was just Anna— suffering from insomnia, possibly, or too nervous to sleep in the dark. The lights woke me up, though, and I couldn't get back to sleep until I'd closed the curtains to block them.

My cats continued to stare at the house. Dusty seemed especially wary. I tried to ply her with treats and cuddles, but she either ignored them or hissed at me. I hated having my cats upset; it felt like a failure on my part for not looking after them better.

But what could I do about a *house*?

As I made a cup of tea, I stared at Anna's doll perched on the windowsill. The dress-clad figure sat with its back to the glass. That bothered me. I knew I would hate having Marwick behind me, lurking where I couldn't see it, so I pulled the kitchen's blinds closed. As I returned to my drink, it struck me that I'd mimicked my other neighbours. They'd all closed the windows facing the Marwick house, too.

I stirred the teabag around in the cup. My limbs felt heavy, and my head was sore. Although I'd slept through the night, I felt like I needed another eight hours. *I've been indoors for too long. I should visit the library again or go to the park or even take a bus trip into town…anywhere to get me into fresher air.*

Three sharp raps came from the front door. I dropped my teabag into the sink. My first thought was to ignore it. I didn't want to see Anna that day, and especially not so early. But that was a horrible sentiment. I didn't dislike Anna; I disliked the house, and if I hated just being near the building, how much worse was it for her living inside? She needed a friend.

I dragged myself down the hallway and opened the door. An unfamiliar man stood outside.

He wasn't as tall as Lukas, but he was heavier. He wore a clean shirt, and his dark hair was combed back, so slick with either water or gel that I could see lines of scalp between the rows. He smelt like cigarette smoke and didn't look pleased to see me.

"Is Anna here?" His voice was brusque and sharp.

I opened my mouth to tell him to try next door then, with a jolt, remembered my promise. I cleared my throat. "Who?"

"Anna. Anna Burrell." Irritation flitted over his features.

I deliberately kept my face blank as I shrugged. "Sorry, no one by that name here."

He rubbed a hand across his mouth, his dark eyes darting over my shoulder to peer inside my home. "She might be going by another name, like Anna Coombs."

"I don't know any Annas. You've got the wrong address."

I tried to close the door, but his arm shot out to hold it open. He was taller than me, and I don't think it was accidental that he appeared to loom. "It's very important that I find her. I'm afraid she may be in trouble. She listed this house as her business address. She could be going under a different first name, too." Again, his eyes flitted over my shoulder, as though he expected to see her hiding in the hallway. "Anna makes dolls. She's small with light hair and blue eyes. She would have moved in within the last few weeks. Do you know anyone, anyone at all, who you think matches that description?"

"No." My mind was screaming, but I met his gaze unflinchingly. I put my hands on the door and the wall so that he wouldn't see them shake. "No one else lives here. But if you ever do find this Anna, please tell her not to use my address. I don't appreciate unsolicited calls."

He puckered his lips in frustration. His dark eyes continued to search my face, so I set my jaw and levelled a glare back at him. He released the door and stepped back. "Fine. Sorry for taking up your time."

I locked the door as soon as it closed and pressed my back to the cool wood. I felt as though I'd been exposed to a fire—something dangerous, wild, and burning within the confines of a pit, but desperate to break out.

The window beside the door overlooked the street. I tweaked the corner of the curtain back and peered through. The man walked towards a red sports car parked in the opposite gutter but stopped part way across the street.

Don't come back. I won't answer the door.

He turned towards Anna's house.

No. How? Did he see her through the window?

I scurried into the kitchen to get a better view, grabbing the wall phone as I passed it. The curtain obscured the house's side, so I yanked it up, not worried if the man saw me, and leaned over the bench to get close to the glass.

He'd stopped at the start of Marwick's driveway, next to the mailbox. Anna had placed a large blue pot there the day before. He stared at it for a long time. Then he lifted his eyes towards Anna's house. I poised my fingers over the phone's buttons, even though the police always took too long to respond to requests about the Marwick house.

The man lingered on the driveway for close to ten minutes, not moving, just staring. I matched his intensity with my own glare, daring him to take even a single step onto Anna's private property. Finally, he spat on the ground then turned and strode back to his car.

I only relaxed when the bright-red vehicle had disappeared past the end of the street. I hung the phone back on its cradle and ran my hands through my hair. I was shaking, but I didn't know why.

Did Anna see him? Her workroom is in the back half of the house.

I jogged to the hallway and tugged my coat on. Our street was so safe that I normally left the door unlocked, but I deliberately pulled the bolt as I left.

Duke crouched among the petunias hedging a house across the street. He rose and trotted across the road as he saw me, tail quivering to signal he wanted pats, but he came to a halt a few feet shy of the border to Marwick House. I held out my hand to invite him forward, but he sat and curled his tail around his feet, his big gold eyes watching me warily. I thought I heard his grumbling growl reverberate.

"Fine, be that way." I half walked, half ran to Anna's front door and knocked a little more harshly than I'd intended. Then

I turned and watched the street just in case the red sports car returned.

Footsteps echoed through the house, and I heard the groan of the staircase's wood flexing. Then the door opened, and Anna stood in the entryway, her hair a mess and smudges of paint over her chin. She looked genuinely surprised to see me. "Jo!"

"Hey." I felt too rattled for niceties. "A guy just came by my house, asking for you. I told him I didn't know you, like you asked, but as he was leaving, he stopped and stared at that pot for ages." I waved towards the letterbox. "Is that…okay?"

I already knew it wasn't. Her face had fallen as I spoke, and terror lit up her blue eyes. As I mentioned the pot, she clasped her hands to her head and moaned.

"No, no, I'm such an idiot, I—"

"All right, it's okay. Tell me what to do."

"It's Raul. He knows. He'll remember the pot. I'm such an idiot. I've got to—I've got to—" She pushed past me and ran down the driveway.

I followed at a distance. "What do you want me to do, Anna? Can I call someone?"

"No." She grabbed the pot's edge and began dragging it towards the house. It was heavy and dug up clumps of the long-dead grass. I hurried to grab the other side, and together, we lifted it.

"Get it around the back," Anna gasped. "Where no one can see it. I shouldn't have put it out the front. It just looked so bare and dead—"

She'd planted a small shrub in the pot, but its leaves were already curling and brown.

We staggered under the planter's weight as we carried it down the side of the house, and finally dropped it beside the back door. We were both breathing heavily from the exertion. Anna collapsed onto the back step and put her head in her hands.

Sitting next to Anna, I tried not to look at the mound of small bones, still visible at the end of the yard. "He's your ex?" I guessed.

She nodded. "Raul." She lifted her head and wiped tear tracks off her cheeks. Her lips were white and her eyes rimmed red. "I don't want to ever see him again. But he's…he's obsessive. He wants to own me. I knew he'd look for me when I left. That's why I was so desperate to get a house quickly; he's the kind of guy who would stake out the women's shelters—but I didn't think he'd find me this easily."

"You should get a restraining order," I said.

"Got one. The problem with restraining orders is they can only help you *after* they've been breached."

"Oh." I took a closer look at her. A hint of discolouration was visible on her forearm where the cardigan had slipped down. My stomach turned over. "Can you move to a different house?"

"No." She stared at the ground ahead of her, but her voice was hollow. "Can't afford to. I spent everything I'd saved on a deposit for this place. Even if I could sell it—and I doubt I could, if it had been on the market for eight months before I found it—it won't be enough to get me any other sort of safe house."

I scuffed my shoes together. "He doesn't know you live here for certain."

"He recognised the pot."

"Yes, but I bet lots of people have pots like that. And he left, which means he has enough uncertainty not to confront you."

She rubbed the back of her hand over her nose. "He'll come back. I know him. I lived with him for five years. Once he decides he wants something, he won't give up until he gets it."

I couldn't think of anything to say for a moment. I wished I could have done more—called the police while he was still there or punched him. *Something.* At last I said, "Safety in numbers. I can stay with you tonight."

"You don't have to do that."

"Sure I do. We'll lock up the house so that it's safe then watch some movies and gossip and paint our nails. It'll be like a classic school sleepover, except with weapons close to hand and the police on speed dial."

Anna laughed, and some of the worry digging into my chest relaxed. "Thanks, Jo. You're a good friend."

Friend. I looked at the pile of bones and tried not to let sinking dread dig its claws into me. *Yeah, I guess we're friends.*

CHAPTER 7

NEITHER ANNA NOR I owned guns, so we improvised. I brought over a baseball bat I'd found in my storage room, along with a Bundt cake I'd baked the day before. We went through the Marwick house together, locking and bolting the doors and making sure the latches on the windows were secure. We closed the blinds and turned off the lights to make it appear as if no one were home, then Anna and I brewed two cups of tea and climbed the stairs to get to her workroom.

The house felt wholly different at night. The shadows were thick over the walls and ceilings, and every creak and groan sounded magnified. The watercolour paintings, all slightly lopsided or twisted, appeared increasingly baleful in the dark.

Anna seemed to have gained confidence in her days of living in the Marwick house alone. Instead of following me, she led the way down the hallway. She moved with assurance, and I wondered what it must have been like pacing the halls alone so many evenings in a row.

The workroom was changed since I'd last seen it. Anna had fixed temporary shelves along the walls, and they all held dolls in various states of being redesigned. Some were still in their original forms—large eyes, garish makeup, and too-long lashes. Others had been stripped of their embellishments. They sat, their faces still holding the ridges and valleys that a face should, but with no eyes or mouths. I tried not to stare at them, even though it felt as if they were staring blindly at me.

A couple of completed dolls waited on the shelf beside Anna's desk. Their smiles were warm, their new eyes bright and shining, and their hair braided or cut and tied into ponytails.

"You've been busy." Uncertain where to put my cup, I held it in my hands as I sat in the spare seat beside the desk.

"Got to pay the bills." Anna laughed then sobered. "Especially now. The dolls sell quickly. I can't keep up with demand, so I've just been pouring myself into this work every waking hour."

I looked over her desk. Half-made outfits were scattered along one side, and a palette with semi-dried paint lay on the other. A recommissioned Barbie rested in the centre of the table, her whites and irises painted in, without pupils, lids, or eyebrows yet. "Did you want to keep working? I have a book in my bag. I don't mind having a quiet evening."

"Are you sure?" Anna glanced at the dolls. "It would be a huge help. I mean, if Raul's found me, I want to complete as much work as quickly as possible."

"Sure." I pulled my novel out of my bag, but I only pretended to read. I was more interested in watching Anna paint.

She worked steadily but with pin-perfect precision. I could tell she'd been doing it for a while. A dab of black went into the centre of each iris to create a pupil. Then dark brown created the eyelids and a little fold above the eyes. She then changed paintbrushes, squeezed out new paint, and worked on the eyebrows, layering different colours to create a natural-looking brow. Finally, once the pupil was mostly dry, she used a toothpick to add a tiny spot of white to each eye, making it sparkle.

I hadn't expected the work to be so fiddly or so difficult. I knew there was no way I could get the dolls' faces as tidy as Anna did. "You must have been a painter before," I said.

She saw me watching, and her ears turned pink. "Yes. My mother taught me. She wanted me to make a living from it. I suppose, in some ways, I am. But after my mother died, I moved in with Raul and…everything sort of fell apart."

I put away the book and leaned forward to indicate I was listening. Anna placed the repainted doll onto a shelf and took up one without a face. She was silent for a moment as she stared at the horribly blank mask, then she squeezed out new tan and red paint to mix a shade for the doll's lips.

"He was amazing at first. Charming and sweet and so devoted to me. I thought he was perfect. Literally a prince charming out of a storybook." She laughed. "I should have realised he was too good to be true. But he was able to keep up that act for so long, and I was smitten with him, and it seemed like a smart idea to move in with him and share the cost of rent and utilities.

"Then he started to control what I did and when. It was such a subtle change that I didn't notice it happening. 'Do you really want to go out with your friends when we could watch a movie together?' or 'Don't get a haircut. I like your hair long.' 'You embarrass yourself when you drink too much, so maybe you shouldn't go to the club anymore.'"

She laughed. It was a bitter, regretful sound. "It's an almost identical story to what a lot of the other girls at the shelter went through. These guys don't love you—they love to control you. And they're so careful about closing the trap an inch at a time that you don't realise it's happening until it's too late to get out. Until he's pushed a wedge between you and your friends. Until he's disconnected you from your community…from anyone who might be willing to help…" She rubbed at her wrist, and I thought again of the bruise I'd seen. She'd been away from Raul for some time. I wondered if it wasn't simply a bruise but the result of a fracture.

"Anyway…" Anna's voice brightened. She bent low over the doll to paint the white teeth inside its lips. "The dolls were the one hobby he let me have, because I didn't need to leave the house to do it, and I think he liked the money. He didn't realise I was siphoning off part of each sale into a secret account. It was enough for a deposit for this house. The banks were wary of lending to me, but one of the ladies at the shelter had a connection who helped me out. This house has been my salvation. So I can forgive some of its quirks."

I lifted my eyebrows. "Quirks? Like…" I chose my words carefully. "Like the sort of stuff that made previous families leave?"

She gave me a shy glance before refocussing on the doll. "I don't want to say supernatural. Because there's nothing that can't be explained as just a coincidence or a fault with the building's design. But yeah, some stuff has been happening."

Curiosity was killing me. I raised my eyebrows even higher and leaned forward.

Anna laughed. "Don't look at me like that. It's nothing spectacular. Like you said, nothing like the stuff you see in Hollywood films. But sometimes, the lights come on by themselves."

"Oh! I've seen that. I thought it was you."

"Sorry. I hope they haven't been keeping you awake. I don't usually find them until morning." She paused to blow on the wet paint to dry it. "Sometimes, I'll be certain that I closed a door, but when I pass it later in the day, it's open again. Or the opposite…open doors will be shut. And once, two days ago, the bathroom taps turned on by themselves. I heard them and shut them off before they flooded the bathroom, but it scared me pretty badly."

I looked about the room. It no longer seemed as safe or as brightly lit as before. The multitude of dolls stared down at me from their shelves, some sightless, some with beady eyes that seemed to glitter. "Do…do you think your house *is* haunted?"

She didn't speak for a very long time. I began to wonder if she'd heard my question, then she took a quick breath. "Perhaps. But if it is, I don't mind so far. I don't think it's a mean ghost."

She had finished the doll's face. She put it aside and picked up the first one again, turning it under her desk lamp to check that the paint had dried and the features were even. Then she flipped it over, took up a pair of bone scissors from the pen jar, and fixed the blades around the doll's ankle. She scrunched up her face as she strained. The foot popped off.

I made an involuntary noise of horror, and Anna stared at me. "Sorry. I didn't mean to startle you. All of these dolls are on their toes to accommodate high heels, but I like to give them comfy shoes before they go to their new family."

"Sure. That makes sense." My voice came out as a squeak. I hated seeing it, but I couldn't look away as she cut off the doll's other foot. It looked too real—too human—with its new face for me to not cringe.

Anna had a tiny pair of sneakers ready. She added glue to their insides then poked the doll's stump legs into the opening. She turned it over to check that they were on straight then leaned back as she held the shoes in place, waiting for the glue to dry.

"My mum lost her feet," I said, surprising even myself. Anna stared at me, and I shrugged. "Diabetes. She wouldn't take her medicine or cut down on the sugar."

"Oh. Oh no, I'm so sorry." Anna looked at the doll in horror. "I didn't think—"

"No, it's fine, I'm over it now. Mostly." I chuckled. "She did it to herself. She passed away four years ago, and I moved here afterwards. It was a good change. Life is better now."

It was the first time I'd thought about my mother—and about

the little white jar I kept in the back of my kitchen cupboards—in a long time.

Anna took her hands away from the shoes, tested that they were set, and put the doll back on its shelf.

A door groaned open.

I swivelled to face the hallway, but Anna didn't move.

"They do that sometimes," she said as she picked up two pieces of cloth and opened a box full of thread. "I try not to worry about it. It could be the wind or even just a crooked doorframe."

Or something more. The phrase hung unspoken between us. I couldn't take my eyes off the hallway. "Do you mind if I…"

"Take a look?" She smiled. "Of course, go for it. I never find anything, though."

CHAPTER 8

THE HALLWAY SEEMED FAR longer than it had before. Shadows and cobwebs clung about the light fittings in equal measure. I moved forward, holding my breath, searching for any sign of motion or soft sound.

The hallway doors were open. I couldn't stop myself from glancing through them as I passed, a little afraid of what I might see. Anna had cleared out the bedrooms that had been inhabited by the previous family. Bare mattresses rested on bedframes, and wardrobe doors stood open, their insides impossibly dark. They felt sadder and colder without the toys scattered over the floor.

The other rooms had been left untouched. Dust dulled the furniture, probably the same furniture they'd held when the house's first family had moved in. Wingback chairs and ottomans clustered amongst wooden side tables and bureaus. It was easy to imagine people from another lifetime sitting at them, hands folded in their laps, perfectly silent as they waited for the hours to progress.

Stop it. I tried to swallow, and a lump caught in my throat. I reached the end of the hallway and faced the curving staircase leading towards the foyer. My fingertips brushed the top of the bannister, the same place touched by countless other visitors, then my heart leapt into my throat as I heard a single, soft, low note.

The piano. I glanced towards the workroom. Glowing golden light spilt through the doorway. I couldn't see Anna, but her movements cast dancing shadows across the ceiling and walls as she sewed an outfit.

I extended one foot down the stairs, then another. My lungs burned with the need to breathe, but fear squeezed my throat closed. I kept close to the walls, afraid of leaning too far over the bannisters, and felt the distorted animal eyes on my back.

The silence in the foyer was almost deafening. The unnatural stillness was heavy—thick enough to taste and solid enough to feel. I turned the corner into the piano's room and felt for its light.

The beautiful, long drapes shifted in a breeze. I stared at them, fear spiking my pulse. There couldn't be any wind. Anna and I had closed every window. I'd fastened the latches in this room myself.

The drapes stilled. I stepped towards them, my hand held outwards to feel the air. It was calm and cool. I looked at the piano. The wood machine still held its cloak of dust. The seat had been untouched. I bent close to the keys and exhaled. Tiny flecks of grey powder flurried away in my breath. The keys hadn't been disturbed, as far as I could see.

I straightened and rotated to watch the room. The curtains stayed still. The doorways empty. The floor's groaning boards undisturbed.

There was something *here, though.* My heart thundered. *Did I actually come into contact with Marwick's ghost?*

I imagined telling Lukas about it, and his voice flashed through my mind, his trademark sarcasm acidic. "Wow, you saw a curtain move, huh? That must have been traumatic. Do you think you'll need counselling?"

But I heard and saw things that are unexplainable. Lukas might not have been excited by my experience, but I knew Anna would be. I retraced my steps to the foyer, turning out the light as I went. *There really was something here.*

The first step creaked as it took my weight. I looked towards the staircase's top, and my heart skipped a beat. A woman sat on the final step, hunched over, long black hair obscuring her face and blending into her slate-grey dress.

I looked again. The woman was gone. In her place, wooden cladding ran up the walls, and shadows from the bannister created strange lines in the dim light. But that didn't calm the pounding in my veins. I tried to speak, but my call escaped as a croak. I licked my lips and tried again. "Anna?"

"Yes?" A door creaked as she moved into the hallway.

"Anna, can we stay downstairs tonight?"

She sounded surprised but not unhappy. "Sure. Easier than trying to carry a mattress into my room, I guess. Just give me a moment to finish these trousers."

I waited, breath suspended, my eyes fixed on the space where I thought I'd seen the woman. The longer I looked, the more foolish I felt. It was a dark corner of the house. It would be easy for a mind to twist the shadows into a human shape.

Still, I felt too exposed. I backed up until my shoulder blades touched the front door, then folded my arms around my chest. Anna was so quiet and took so long to appear that I'd started mustering my courage to go upstairs in search of her.

"Done! Sorry for making you wait!" She appeared at the top of the stairs, standing where I thought I'd seen the woman. Her eyes shone in the moonlight coming through the windows. "I've got that doll dressed, at least. It was a good night of work."

"Great." My voice croaked. I wanted to warn her—to tell her about what I'd seen—but the words died before they reached my lips. Truthfully, I wasn't sure *what* I'd seen. And Anna wouldn't get any benefit from fearmongering.

She skipped down the stairs and stopped at my side. "Jo, you look pale."

"Just scaring myself." I gave her a weak smile.

She laughed and threaded her arm through mine. "And I thought *I* was the scaredy cat. How about we make some hot chocolate?"

"That sounds nice." I looked back at the stairs a final time. No figures appeared there. The steps were lit by a golden glow flowing down the length of the hallway. "Did you want to turn off the workroom light?"

She gave me an odd look. "I did."

We both looked towards the hallway. Anna's enthusiasm ebbed as she saw the light. She squeezed my arm and resolutely fixed her smile back into place. "I'll turn it off later."

I relaxed once we were in the kitchen and had the noise of the kettle to keep us company. We took chairs at opposite sides of the bench and cut into the Bundt cake I'd brought. I told Anna about the moving curtains.

She looked thoughtful then said, "Maybe you disturbed the air when you opened the door?"

"Yeah, probably." Had the music room door already been open when I went in? I thought it had.

"Hey, Jo, can I ask a question?" Anna was spooning cocoa powder into mugs. She wouldn't meet my eyes.

"Sure. Questions never hurt anyone."

"Earlier, you said things have gotten better since you moved here. Did you have trouble with your family, too?"

My mind's eye flashed to the white jar I kept in the back of my kitchen cupboard. "Sort of."

"That man who visited you the other day. The tall one. You said he was your cousin, but you didn't sound happy about it." She snuck a glance at me. "Is he…a problem?"

"Oh." I realised where her mind was going. "No, Lukas is fine. I mean, he's a cynical jerk, but as far as family goes, he's not too bad. He's the only one who really, genuinely cared about what happened to me when my mother died. His mother—my aunt—always took my mother's side." I scrunched my face up. "I don't know why."

Anna rose to fill the cups with boiling water and milk but kept her eyes on me.

I stared at my cake. I'd never really had a chance to talk about it with anyone, not even Lukas. It felt like picking at an old scab: painful and possibly unhealthy but still very satisfying. "I know now that my mother was a narcissist. It helps me understand some of the things she did. And why she was...like *that*. She needed attention to live, and it didn't matter who or what she hurt to get it."

Anna put my cup in front of me then sat down. She folded her hands over the table.

I watched the swirling chocolatey milk as its bubbles popped one at a time. "I was an accessory to her. When I did something well, she never praised me but always bragged about it to her friends. Like an excuse to show off what a great mother she was. When I did something wrong, she complained about me instead. *What did I do to deserve this wild, unruly child? Why is she doing this to me?*" I'd inadvertently mimicked the whine my mother had adopted when she was unhappy. It made me want to cry, so I smiled instead. "Then she was diagnosed with diabetes, and let me tell you, I'd never seen her so happy before. It was like her golden ticket for never-ending attention. She didn't want to get better; she wanted to have a condition to exploit for sympathy, and exploit it, she did. She'd make every bad choice she could then gush about how difficult her life was and how badly she was suffering."

Anna propped her chin up in her hands. "That sounds tough."

"I was too young to realise how unhealthy it was. She lost her legs below the knee. Instead of trying to use a wheelchair, she decided she should be bedbound, and I had to move back in to look after her." There was a lot more I wanted to tell Anna: About walking past my mother's bedroom door and hearing her on the phone to her friends, telling them that I neglected her. About being woken by screams in the middle of the night and rushing to her room only to find she was bored and lonely. About how she would fake incontinence to punish me if I went too long without checking in on her. About the note she'd written before her suicide. But the words died on my tongue. Reliving that part of my life wouldn't help anyone, least of all me.

I took a deep breath and tried to clear the air. "Anyway, after her funeral, I decided I needed to get away from that side of the family entirely. I moved out here. Lukas still visits me, which is nice, but otherwise, I'm happy with just myself and my cats." I sipped my drink. "People are too complicated."

Anna chuckled and held her cup out. "Amen."

"We hermits should stick together." I clinked my cup with hers. "I know that's a contradiction, but…"

"It makes sense."

We shared a grin. I'd forgotten what it felt like to have friends. I liked it a lot, and I felt bad for avoiding Anna over the previous days. So what if her house was strange? She was worth it. I tried to remember the phrase she'd used on the day I'd met her: *Sometimes you need to make sacrifices for good things.*

We made up our beds on the living room couches. The seats were old but surprisingly soft, and we pushed them next to each other so that we could both watch the TV. Anna didn't own any movies, but the previous family had left their collection. We bypassed the horror films, settled on a comedy, then snuggled into our beds to laugh for a few hours.

Anna fell asleep before the movie finished. I turned off the TV during the credits and lay in the dark, staring up at the ceiling and listening to the house's silence. Sometime after midnight, I heard a car pass the house. The air was quiet for a handful of minutes, then another car passed. Shortly after, a third followed.

I tried to tell myself they were different vehicles, all with their own reasons for disturbing the quiet at such a late hour, and not a red sports car circling the block.

CHAPTER 9

I SHRUGGED SLEEP AWAY. Moonlight came through the thin curtains, giving Marwick House an ethereal blue glow. I blinked fogginess out of my eyes and sat up.

Someone was playing a lullaby on the piano. The tune was slow. Ponderous. It repulsed me. It sounded full of regret and broken dreams, almost like a dirge.

Anna still slept in the couch next to me. She'd curled both hands around the base of her throat, but her breathing was slow and even.

I felt like I was walking through a dream. I stood carefully, my bare feet digging into the carpet, which needed a good vacuum to get rid of the dust. The tune, steady and grim, floated through the house. I wanted it to stop. More than wanted... I *needed* it to stop before it suffocated me.

The floorboards creaked as I crossed into the foyer. The big wall clock ticked, but it seemed out of beat, as though its seconds had been dragged out twice as long as they should have been. I stepped towards the music room. The door was closed. I'd left it open earlier, hadn't I? The wood groaned when I pushed on it. The piano fell silent. Its last notes hung in the air, incomplete but insistent. I pressed my hands over my ears to block out the reverberations. They faded gradually. I began to breathe again.

A soft hiccupping, wailing noise came from the second floor. I looked towards the ceiling. It sounded like a baby crying.

I need to wake Anna.

My skin prickled as I stepped back into the foyer. As I passed the stairs, the child's cries were joined by a new sound: the jangle of chain links clinking together.

The rattle sent icy fear into my core. I froze, staring up the staircase, my eyes hunting for motion amongst the shadows. I knew where the sounds came from. They echoed out of the blue room at the end of the hall, with its slate-grey curtains and eyeless dolls.

The infant's cries softened then ceased. The chains continued to clink. My mouth tasted like sandpaper. I pressed my sweaty palms into my pyjama pants. It wasn't my imagination that the chains were growing closer. Any moment, I would see a figure walk out of the hallway and pause at the top of the stairs, an infant clasped to her chest.

Then the chains made a sharp, inharmonious noise. They'd been pulled taut. The figure didn't appear. Instead, her voice drifted down to me. She'd begun to sing a lullaby.

I pressed my hands over my ears again. The tune was familiar; it had come from the piano just a moment before. Miserable. Grim. Then the tune swelled, and the sadness broke into anger.

My throat was too tight to breathe. I staggered back into the lounge room and slammed the door behind me. "Anna. Anna, wake up!"

I rounded the lounge chair. Anna had rolled onto her back. Her eyes were open, staring blindly at the ceiling, and her lips were parted a fraction. Her hair had been mussed, strands lying over her face and tangled across the chair's armrest.

Blood ran from the back of her head, staining the blue pillows brown and dripping off the cushions and onto the carpet. Tiny bone fragments washed out with the gore. Her skull had been broken open like an egg.

He got her. I left her alone—and Raul got her—

I couldn't think. Couldn't breathe. My legs lost their strength, and I fell to my knees as a scream rose in my chest.

Anna's blank eyes flicked towards me. Her lips twitched. "What's wrong, Jo?"

The voice didn't belong to Anna. It had been distorted into a crackling, gurgling slur. Somehow, the words fell perfectly in time with the morbid lullaby coming from the second floor. I tried to scream at Anna to stay away from me, but she was moving, sitting up, a line of bright-red blood trickling over her open lips—

Then suddenly the scene changed. It was like flipping a light switch. The blood bathing Anna's head and dress were gone. Her skull was intact. Her hair was tidy again.

I couldn't escape the terror and clutched my hands across my chest defensively.

Her eyes narrowed in concern. "What's wrong? Did you see something, Jo?"

"I…I…" The lullaby had faded. The awful, heavy dread saturating the room vanished. I took a quick breath and found I was covered in sweat.

"Was it a nightmare?" She reached towards me, but I recoiled. "Jo, you're scaring me. What happened?"

"Just a dream," I choked, because that was what it had to be. "Just…just a bad dream."

She watched me for another second, worrying at her lip, then stood to turn on the lights. The room didn't seem so awful without its shadows. "Are you sure? You look awful, Jo—you really scared me."

"Scared myself," I managed and choked through a horrified laugh.

Anna helped me back into my chair and wrapped a blanket around my shoulders. She offered to make me another hot chocolate, but I begged her to stay in the room with me. I still didn't feel safe with letting her out of my sight.

She returned to her chair and sat cross-legged. "Do you want to talk about it? Sometimes, discussing bad dreams helps—"

"No, definitely not." I felt nauseous. A car engine purred down the street, and I flinched. The headlights glided past our window then disappeared.

Not a sports car. Not Raul. Please.

Anna ran her hands through her hair. I stared at the motion, still afraid of seeing the locks saturated with blood and bone fragments, but the only thing that caught her fingers was a tangle.

"I'm sorry for making you stay tonight." She dropped her hands back into her lap. "I know you don't like this house. Did you want to head home?"

"No." I pressed my hand to my heart, willing it to slow, then spoke in a softer voice. "Thanks, but it was just a bad dream. I want to stay. Besides, human company will be better than snoring cats."

She chuckled. "All right."

A car passed again. That was too many for coincidence. I rose and crossed to the window to tweak the curtain back. Our road didn't have streetlights, and I couldn't see anything except a patch of dead lawn.

"Maybe I will take you up on that offer of hot chocolate." I'd said it partially to distract Anna from the car and partially as an excuse to stay up a little longer. I didn't think I could sleep any time soon. "I'll come with you."

"That's all right. You stay here and rest. I'll bring it back."

"No, please, let me come."

She nodded, so we both went into the kitchen, turning on the light as we went. I twitched as I heard a jangling noise, thinking the chains had returned, but it was only Anna pulling cups out of the cupboard.

It must have been a dream…right? The sensations and sounds had seemed so real. I could still remember the tune well enough to hum it. I sat at the bench and fiddled with a napkin to give my fingers something to do.

Anna kept sending me quick glances. She was worrying at her lip again. I tried to smile while I counted beats and hoped my heart rate would slow to match them. It didn't. My fingers trembled when I reached for the cup Anna handed me.

"How about we put on another movie?" she asked. "Something fun and distracting."

"That would be gr—"

The car passed our house again. The purring motor escalated my nerves, making me nearly crazed in my fear and frustration. I slammed the mug down.

"Jo?" Anna followed me as I strode back into the foyer. I hit the light switch, unbolted the front door, and threw it open.

I squinted to see through the darkness. A splash of colour lurked under the tree on the opposite side of the street. Then tyres screeched as the red sports car sped away. I swore under my breath.

"Jo?"

Anna huddled beside the staircase, trying to stay out of sight. I shut the door. "Sorry. I didn't mean to… Sorry."

"It's okay." Her smile was fragile.

I tried to coax my shaking fingers to turn the lock, but it took me a few seconds to succeed. When I turned back, the woman stood behind Anna. It was a perfect, horrible image. Anna had her arms wrapped around herself as she leaned her shoulder against the staircase's side. Her head was tilted, her fine hair falling about her shoulders, and her blue eyes wide.

The woman in grey stood behind her, head bowed, her face impossible to see behind the tangle of black hair falling over it. She held her pose stiffly, looking down at the girl in front of her. Mottled fingers curled over Anna's shoulder.

I opened my mouth, but the figure was gone before I could make a noise. Only Anna remained, shivering, with a clot of black shadows hanging behind her.

"We need to go." The words left me as a rasp. "There's... there's something here. We need to go to my house."

Anna glanced over her shoulder. She examined the place where the woman had stood, but when she turned back, her face only held confusion. "What did you see?"

"A woman. A ghost. I think." My throat was tight. I swallowed and held my hand towards Anna. "Come on. We need to go. I don't think it's safe here."

She hesitated a second but then took my hand and let me lead her through the door and down the rotting, peeling porch. I was grateful. I couldn't spend another moment in Marwick House, and I didn't want my friend there, either.

Duke sauntered out of the shrubs lining the front of my property as we neared. He yawned and stretched then matched our pace as we hurried to my home. I sent him a warning look: *Stay away from that house.*

But I didn't need to tell him. He'd known that all along.

CHAPTER 10

ANNA SLEPT CURLED ON my lounge, a blanket tucked tightly around her and her hands balled under her chin. I stayed awake and alert in the seat opposite. If I looked to my right, I could watch the side of her house through the window. At first, I'd closed the curtains to block the view, but that was somehow worse, like having a gigantic spider on the bedroom wall…and then looking away for a second and not being able to find it again.

I'd ended up pulling open the curtains and turning on the small desk lamp beside my chair. The light was enough to stop the darkness from swallowing me but not so bright that it woke Anna. Dusty leapt into my lap around four in the morning and curled up there. I buried my hands in her fur as we watched the Marwick house together.

One of Marwick's upstairs lights turned on shortly before

THE HOUSE NEXT DOOR

four thirty. I glared at the golden glow, searching for movement inside, but the room seemed empty.

The car didn't return. I hoped I'd startled Raul enough by bursting out of the house to chase him off. I was different enough from Anna that he wouldn't have confused me for her, even in the dark. If we were lucky, he would think he'd been wrong that Anna lived there and not come back. It was wishful thinking, but I needed something good to cling to.

Dawn eventually broke and shattered the hold fear had claimed over me during the night. I dozed off watching the sunrise and didn't wake for hours. When I did, I was alone: Dusty had left me, and Anna was no longer sleeping on the couch. She'd folded the blanket into a tidy square.

"Anna?" I jolted out of my chair, and a stiff muscle in my neck made me flinch. "Anna, are you here?"

I jogged through my house, checking the kitchen, the bathrooms, and finally the upstairs rooms. Anna wasn't there, but when I looked through my bedroom window, I saw the upstairs light in Marwick House had been turned off. I muttered furiously as I ran back down the stairs and burst outside.

Anna must have heard my door slam, because she came out of Marwick House as I neared the fence. We came to a halt with the grey pickets dividing us, me breathing heavily, she wearing a sheepish smile.

"Sorry, I didn't want to wake you," she said.

I waved at Marwick House. "Why'd you go back? I saw stuff in there last night—"

"I know." She rubbed at the back of her neck. "And I believe you. I promise. But…it's my house; there's no point in hiding from it. I don't have anywhere else to stay."

"You can stay with me." I was talking too quickly, but the words wouldn't stop. "I've got room. You don't have to go back there."

"Jo, thank you. I appreciate it. I really do." She sighed and squeezed my forearm. "But I want to be independent. After Raul…I want my own place, one that I own, one that I can look after. And even if this house is…is…"

Haunted, I thought.

Instead, she said, "*Peculiar*, even so, it's *mine*. And I don't think it wants to hurt me. Is there anything wrong with a peculiar house if it's friendly?"

I opened my mouth. The image of Anna's skull smashed open appeared behind my eyes, but it didn't seem right to tell her about it. The image had been a dream brought on by stress; imposing my own nightmares on Anna would be unhelpful at best and manipulative at worst. "I just don't want to see you get hurt."

"I think I'll be fine." She grinned. "Thanks for staying with me last night. I really needed it. But I'm feeling better today. I'm feeling…I don't know, safer. More confident. I think I can make this work. I *want* to make this work."

"Okay." I slumped onto the fence. The remnants of the previous night's anxiety still hung over me like a cloud. "Maybe you're right. Maybe there's nothing dangerous there. But…do you mind if we take some precautions anyway?"

"I love precautions." She laughed. "My life is a whole series of precautions stacked on top of each other. Tell me what to do, and I'll do it."

"Take my phone number first. If you see anything weird, give me a call."

She pulled a pen out of her pocket, and I recited my number. She wrote it on her palm.

I ran my fingers through my hair as I tried to think. "And…I'd like to do some research on the house. Maybe knowing its history will help us understand why it's like this."

"That's a good idea."

"All right. Good." I released a breath. "Stay safe, okay? You can always crash at my place if you need to."

"Thanks again, Jo." She looked genuinely happy. "Raul aside, I feel like I'm actually starting to get my life together."

That makes one of us. I drummed my fingers on the fence as I watched Anna return to her home. I glanced over the street and saw Mr. Korver watching me warily as he watered his plants. His massive bushy eyebrows pulled lower as I turned towards him, and he shuffled around to face away from me.

I looked down. I was still in my cat-print pyjamas. I sighed and hurried back into my house. My cats wove around my legs with escalating impatience while I dished up their food. I made a quick breakfast for myself, showered to get rid of the tacky sweat that had dried over my body, and changed into fresh clothes. Then an idea occurred to me. I went to my room and grabbed the phone off the side table.

"Lukas," he answered after three rings.

I plopped onto the edge of my bed and pulled my feet up under me. "Hey, I have a job for you."

"Oh, hello, Jo. Yes, Mother is well, thank you for asking. Millie's good. I can't complain. How have you been?"

"Come on, Lukas, this is important."

"All right. Fine. What's this job, and will I be paid?"

"I need to borrow your cameras and your brains, and I'll pay you in brownies."

"I'm listening."

He wasn't going to like my proposition. I scrunched up my face. "Okay, so, you know the haunted house next door?"

"Goodbye, Jo."

"No, no! Hang on! Anna, the lady who lives there, she's having some trouble with a stalker ex. I stayed there last night. This guy kept driving by; we were worried he'd try to break into her house."

Lukas was silent for a moment. Then he said, "Sorry, I didn't realise it was a legitimate situation. What do you want me to do?"

"I was hoping you'd have some of those motion-sensor cameras. You know, the ones that ring alarms when someone moves into their view."

"You're thinking of security systems, which is worlds away from my industry."

"Yeah, except neither Anna, nor I have the money to pay for a security system."

He sighed heavily. "I'll ring some friends and see if there's anything we can do. Call you back in twenty."

"Thanks, Lukas."

I dropped the phone as he hung up. I'd only half-lied. The security systems would be useful for ensuring Raul didn't cause trouble, but my main motive for getting them was to see if they caught any sort of paranormal activity.

Lukas took his time calling back. I spent my time pacing across my room, alternately staring out the window at the house next door and fidgeting with the hem of my shirt. When the phone finally rang, I pounced on it.

"Lukas?"

"Hey. Good news. A friend has motion sensors that will connect to my cameras, and he's going to lend them to me. Another friend has some software to set up an alarm and make everything work. I can collect them and be over there in four hours or so."

"Perfect. Bring lots. We want to monitor the inside of the house as well as the exterior."

I could picture Lukas's glare through the phone. "Jo. Please tell me this isn't about ghosts."

"Well, I mean, if we're going to be setting them up, we may as well—"

"Does this crazy stalker ex even exist, or are you just a pathological liar now?"

I bristled. "He *does* exist. And so do the ghosts. I saw one last night."

"Jo."

"No, come on, Lukas. Anna's scared. She's living in that big house all by herself, and she's trying to fight monsters on the outside as well as the inside. She's a classic damsel in distress. Don't guys like that?"

"Jo." He sounded exasperated. "I specialise in experimental and transcendental films exploring the human psyche. If my colleagues find out I'm ghost hunting, they'll never take me seriously again."

"All right, if you won't do it for her, do it for me. You're the closest thing I have to family, and there's no one else I can go to for help."

The silence stretched out for a long gap, then he groaned. "Fine. Manipulative little weirdo. I'll be there in a few hours."

"You're the best. I'll bake you *two* trays of brownies."

"You'd better."

I grinned as I hung up. The cameras might not actually catch anything, but I would sleep a little easier knowing they were there.

That just left one avenue of enquiry: learning Marwick House's history. I turned on my laptop, stretched as it booted up, then typed in the house's address.

There were a lot of results. I scrolled through the list, scanning titles and web pages, and found a disturbing trend. All of the pages were old house listings. Marwick had been changing hands frequently from since long before I'd moved in. Some of the listings were only months apart. Occasionally, an occupant made it a year or a year and a half, but that seemed to be the maximum. My earlier elation faded. If Anna was right—if the spirits inhabiting the building were friendly—what was making the tenants move so often?

Despite the numerous search results, I couldn't find any actual information about the house. It didn't appear on any history sites or haunted location blogs.

I shut down the computer, thought for a moment, then went downstairs. I took a fruitcake out of the cupboard, wrapped it in a cloth, collected my jacket, and stepped through the front door.

CHAPTER 11

PENNY CRAWFORD LIVED ACROSS the street from me. She was notorious for two things: staying in the same house for more than sixty years and knowing everything about everyone's business. Some days, when the curiosity bug bit me, I watched the other houses through my front windows. Almost invariably, I would look towards Penny's house and see her looking right back.

I crossed the street and followed the stone pavers leading to the front door. Penny's house was old-fashioned, and her garden was edging towards being badly overgrown, but the building had charm. She'd supposedly moved in there with her husband when they married, and had never moved out. She had to be at least eighty, but she moved and spoke with the agility of someone half her age.

Penny opened the door before I had a chance to knock. I was fairly certain she'd been watching me come up her driveway, but I didn't make a fuss about it.

"I've got a whole lot of questions and think you might have some answers. Can I come in? I brought cake."

"Of course. Sitting room's through there. In you go, chop-chop." Penny took the cake, pulled out a corner of the cloth to examine it, then nodded in satisfaction. She disappeared into the kitchen.

It wasn't my first time in Penny's sitting room. I'd visited several times in my four years there, most recently when the previous family had fled in the middle of the night. Penny had been the most help out of all of my neighbours…which wasn't saying much. She'd heard the screams, seen the gunshots, and watched the family drive away. But she hadn't called the police and didn't know what had caused them to leave.

The living room's furniture was from another decade. The chairs were all faded floral print with white doilies thrown over them, and a fake fireplace complete with real dust-covered logs decorated the back corner. I admired the curio cabinets filled with fine china until Penny returned, carrying a plate of sliced cake, two teacups, and my folded towel on a tray.

"Go ahead, ask away," she said as she passed me a cup. That was one thing I liked about Penny—she didn't spend time on preambles or waste words.

"Okay, so, the Marwick house. You know a new lady, Anna, moved in, don't you?"

It was a stupid question, and I deserved the scornful look Penny gave me. "You've been quite friendly with her. Visiting often. Sleeping over last night. Well, most of last night, anyway."

Of course she would have seen us leave. It was unreasonable to expect Penny to sleep through the night like a normal human. "Well, I wanted to know about the house's history. I'm trying to find out if it had anything…violent or unsavoury in its past. Something that could be affecting the building now."

"You mean ghosts." That was another thing I liked about Penny—she cut straight to the point and didn't judge the questions. "Certainly. Did you want me to give you the abridged version, or would you like the whole story?"

With three hours until Lukas arrived, it was a no-brainer. "Whole story, please."

"All right." Penny settled back into her seat and picked up her tea. She blew a wisp of steam away before beginning. "Marwick House was one of the first buildings constructed on the street. You might have noticed its architecture is a bit off-theme. The original owner had planned it to be a small hotel, though he tragically died of a stroke before its doors ever opened."

"Oh! What was his name? Do you think—"

"No, I *don't* think he's haunting Marwick House." Penny sent me a sharp glare to silence me. "None of that started until decades later. Let me tell my story."

"Sorry."

"For a while, the building held a couple of respectable, normal families. It was, as I said, off-design for this neighbourhood, but some people thought that provided it with a layer of charm. The house only really developed its reputation as a haunted building when the Marwicks moved in."

I lifted my eyebrows. "So the house was named after them, not the original owner?"

"Correct. And with good reason. They became so notorious that it was impossible to separate the name from the house. In 1942, Ray and Helen Marwick moved into the building. They were a young, recently married couple. Ray had not long come back from the army, having served for only two years, and was considered a catch. Helen was a meek, quiet sort of girl but considered pretty and a good wife. They were the upstanding family everyone else admired. For a few years."

Penny sipped her tea. "My husband and I moved in here shortly after the Marwicks' reputation started to drop. Ray was cruel and controlling of his wife. This was a different time, mind—women weren't supposed to divorce their husbands, and what happened in the home stayed in the home. Helen would stay locked in that house for days or even weeks, and when she was eventually allowed out, Ray always accompanied her. We all felt bad for Helen, but none of us could do anything to help her except invite her over for tea occasionally when her husband was at work."

She paused to sigh deeply, and I leaned forward. "What is it?"

"I was one of the women who used to invite her over. Apparently, her husband didn't approve of it, and when he found out, he went wild. We didn't see her for days, and when she came to church that Sunday, she had bruises all over her arms and face."

I shuddered. "He sounds horrible."

"Oh, he assuredly was. He was charismatic, though, and had a lot of friends who turned a blind eye to his domestic life. Helen didn't deserve what she went through. But she was so quiet that I don't think she knew how to ask for help, even if there was help to give.

"I wish I had a nice ending to this story, but I don't. One night, shortly after eleven, Helen fell from her bedroom window. We don't know if it was accidental, a suicide, or murder. But she cracked her skull open on the stones below. Because the window was at the back of the house, no one saw or heard it happen. Ray rightfully predicted he would be suspected for murder if he called the police, so he did the sensible, rational thing and buried her in the backyard."

"Oh." Nausea surfaced, and I put my cup down. "Do you know where in the yard?"

"I haven't ever seen behind the property. Apparently, it was in one of the corners."

I thought of the animal grave. All those little flecks of white churning out of the brown. If we'd dug deep enough, would we have found human bones?

"Ray tried to tell everyone his wife had gone to visit her cousin. We were naturally suspicious, but again, it was a different time. What could we do? Ask for an address to write to her, then never hear back?"

A grim smile lit up Penny's face. "Helen got her revenge, though. Rumours say her ghost lingered in the house. She tormented her cruel husband. She presented him with awful nightmares, stared at him through his mirror, and rattled chains while he tried to sleep. Four months after he buried Helen, Ray took a length of rope, threw it over the branch of a tree beside her grave, and hung himself."

That confirmed the burial spot. I chewed on the corner of my thumb. "Why didn't Ray move?"

"How would I know? Maybe he was afraid his wife's body would be found. Maybe he couldn't afford to leave. Maybe the idea of moving never occurred to him." Penny snorted. "Whichever way, according to the legend, Helen saw justice from beyond the grave. Ray's body was found when he didn't show up to work on Monday. They cut him down. Someone noticed the ground below him had been disturbed, and the grass hadn't yet covered it again. They dug it up and found Helen's body. Then traces of her blood were found under her bedroom window, and the story was pieced together. It was a media sensation. No one could talk about anything else for weeks afterwards."

"So Helen continues to haunt the Marwick home?"

"Allegedly. Mind, I've never seen or heard anything super-natural in that house. But you've got to say it is remarkable how quickly its residents come and go." Penny broke off a corner of the cake and popped it into her mouth. "If I were in your shoes, I wouldn't get too attached to that new lady. She won't last long."

I thanked Penny and left. She'd given me a lot to mull over, and I spent some time standing on the sidewalk, looking from my own building to Marwick House. The day was cool, and thin cloud cover dimmed the sun. Autumn had finally given way to winter.

I put my hands in my pockets and returned to my home to wait for Lukas.

CHAPTER 12

ALL THREE OF MY cats were hiding. I drifted through my house, searching for some kind of company and comfort, before ending up in my sanctuary, the kitchen. I pulled bowls and spoons out of the cupboard without any idea of what I wanted to cook. I only knew I wanted to make *something*.

Cooking had always been a comfort for me. I'd given it up during the years I'd been looking after my mother—she would have insisted on eating it, and the sugar would have made everything worse—but now that I had freedom, I spent too much time and too much money pouring batters into tins.

I'd promised Lukas brownies, but I wanted to cook them closer to his arrival so that they would still be warm. There was time to make something else first. I shuffled through the cupboards, looking for ingredients to inspire me, while my mind churned over Penny's story. I thought about Helen's life and how isolated and helpless she must have felt, then I pictured the sallow, dark-haired wraith that had appeared behind Anna. I shuddered.

My fingertips landed on a cold porcelain container. I stared at it, shocked that I'd drifted to this cupboard, the one I normally never opened, without even thinking. The little white jar looked so innocent, as though it could have held anything—herbs, tea, sugar. If anyone else saw it, they would never guess its significance. I pulled back and shut the door firmly.

Flour rained from my sieve to create a pillowy mountain in the bowl. I still didn't have a recipe, so I didn't bother measuring ingredients. The cake would be a surprise for everyone, including me. After the flour came sugar. *Brown sugar,* I decided. I wanted something rich and dense and too sweet. Nutmeg, cinnamon, ginger. Baking powder. Cocoa powder. Dried fruit—not enough to make a fruitcake, just something that would create a pop of surprise. I mixed the dry ingredients then went to get the liquids.

Anna's doll still sat on the windowsill. The eyes were too detailed. They looked dead, but at the same time, they followed me. I ignored it the best I could as I collected eggs and milk.

I added the wet ingredients indiscriminately. I didn't feel like creaming eggs and butter, so I didn't. A line had been crossed when I'd mixed cocoa and dried fruit, so I pushed further, adding in any ingredient in my cupboard that caught my fancy. Vanilla extract. Mint. On a whim, I added chilli flakes. *That's what the fancy chefs are doing now, isn't it? Mixing sweet and spicy?* I could do that, too.

The batter was a lumpy, runny mess when I poured it into an

ungreased tin. I didn't care. I threw it into the oven at a too-hot temperature. *Let it burn.*

I pressed my back against the oven's handle, breathing too fast for the energy I'd expended. Cold sweat made me shiver. *What am I doing? Have I gone insane?*

I looked down at my hands. They were smeared with flour and dried vanilla extract. A raised red mark stood out on my index finger. I crossed to the sink, washed my hands clean, and checked again. The small red bump had a dark centre. The splinter from my first day in Marwick was still stuck under my skin. I grumbled to myself and went to find my sewing box. I couldn't believe the wood had been there so long without bothering me before.

The discordant smells of cinnamon and mint essence floated through my kitchen as I settled under the brightest light with a needle. I poked at the splinter, trying to ease it out, but the skin seemed to have melded over it.

"Fine, be stubborn." I gritted my teeth and poked the needle through the skin. Blood welled, hiding the black wood fragment from sight. I kept digging, trying to get under it, trying to even find it. Something warm trickled over my finger and slipped down the back of my hand. My mental agitation manifested in frantic and furious probing. The warmth continued to flow. It dribbled over my wrist and dripped onto the bench. I went deeper.

The doorbell rang, and I snapped out of what felt like a trance. For a second, I couldn't remember what I'd been doing. Then I looked at my hand and choked on a gasp.

Blood flowed from where I'd gouged a hole in my finger. It was everywhere—running over my hand, onto the bench, onto the floor. I ran to the sink and put my hand under the water. Hot pain bloomed from the cut.

The visitor leaned on the doorbell, creating a cacophony of noise through my house.

"I'm coming!" I yelled. I pulled my hand out from under the water. The cut didn't look too large, but it wouldn't stop bleeding. I grabbed a tea towel and bundled it around my hand.

A new alarm joined the blaring doorbell. I looked up. Smoke filled the kitchen; it poured out of the oven in heavy black plumes. I swore and hurried to unlatch the window. When I opened the oven, I nearly choked on the smoke. The cake was scorched black. I didn't understand; it hadn't been cooking for more than ten minutes.

The visitor was knocking now, the bangs growing increasingly urgent. I muttered a swear word, turned off the oven, and ran down the hallway.

"Hold on! I'm coming." I unlatched the door and opened it with my left hand, the right still swaddled in the tea towel.

Lukas stood on the doorstep, his long features grim. "Took you long enough. I was starting to think the cats had eaten you after all."

I pulled a face. "Don't start. I've had a rubbish day. And I wasn't expecting you to get here early."

He gave me an odd look. The smoke alarm continued to wail. Lukas's eyes shifted from the tea towel wrapped around my hand to the hallway, where black smoke rolled along the ceiling. "I'm late, actually. Jo, what happened?"

"Nothing," I said reflexively. "Wait here a moment. I've got to sort my kitchen out."

In typical Lukas fashion, he ignored me and followed me down the hallway. I pulled the cake out of the still-hot oven and threw it on the stovetop. Then I grabbed a chair, dragged it under the smoke alarm, and climbed onto it so that I could reach the source of the blaring beeps.

"It's not like you to burn a cake," Lukas yelled to be heard over the siren. "And what happened to your hand?"

Lies sounded more reasonable than the truth. "I fell asleep holding a knife. The doorbell startled me, and I accidentally cut myself."

Finding the button to turn off the alarm was awkward with one hand swaddled, so I smacked at the battery cover until it popped open. I threw the batteries on the bench. I'd barely gotten off the chair when a second alarm went off in the hallway.

"I'll get it." Lukas grabbed the chair from me, even though I was pretty sure he was tall enough to reach the alarm without it.

I scowled and moved through the lower floor, opening as many windows as I could. My hand ached. I didn't want to take the cloth off to look at it again. The sun had started to set, I realised with a jolt. The afternoon had melted away.

Maybe I really did fall asleep? I was just trying to get the splinter out... I hadn't been at it for more than a minute, tops. Right?

I returned to the kitchen. The burning smell stuck in my nose and throat. I looked at the abomination of a cake I'd made. It was seared black. The top had cracked, and the gorges created a strange pattern. The more I stared at them, the more I began to think they looked like a woman lying down, her head twisted to the side, her arms and legs flung out, one shoe knocked off her foot—

"Jo."

Lukas's voice came from just over my shoulder. I startled. How long had he been standing there? The alarms no longer blared, at least.

To my surprise, he actually smiled. "Do you have a first aid kit?"

"Yeah." I gave the cake a final, wary glance. The fissures no longer created any kind of image. I opened the cupboard under the sink and found my kit, which hadn't seen use since I'd moved in.

"Great." He took it from me and carefully pulled out a chair by the kitchen bench. "Here, have a sit down. I'll look at your hand."

He kept smiling. His voice was kind and soft, not the usual sharp barks he gave me. He sounded as though he were trying to coax a frightened animal out of a corner. It was the same way he'd spoken after my mother died.

I shivered and turned away. The doll continued to stare at me from the windowsill. Her smile had just the right tilt to suggest she'd seen everything that had happened in that kitchen…and was judging me for it. "I'll be fine. I'll just wash it again and—"

"It's okay, Jo. I'm here now. Just sit down, and I'll get that fixed up in a heartbeat."

I hated being coddled, and I hated the patronising concern. He thought I'd had a meltdown. *Maybe I did,* my mind whispered, reminding me of the abomination of dried fruit, cocoa, and mint essence on my bench.

Lukas was waiting, eyebrows lifted, smile firmly in place. He was stubborn, and I knew arguing would only escalate the situation and make him worry more. I took a sharp breath through my nose and grudgingly sat. He peeled the tea towel away from my hand and grimaced. The cloth had become saturated with blood.

"It was such a stupid mistake." I spoke quickly, desperate to convince Lukas that I wasn't crazy or dangerous. "I was just waiting for the cake to cook, and I fell asleep. Good thing you arrived before it burnt any worse."

He dabbed antiseptic over the finger. Fire spread through the cuts, and I clamped my teeth together to keep silent. When he spoke, his voice still held that awful, kind patience. "What sort of cake were you making?"

"An experiment." I prayed he wouldn't notice that the marks in my finger hadn't come from a single blade slice. "You know how chefs have started mixing spices into sweet foods? Chili chocolate and stuff like that? I wanted to try that in a cake. But it's probably a good thing it burnt. I bet it would have tasted awful."

I was talking too quickly and too much. I shut my mouth.

The cut continued to bleed, so Lukas wrapped a clean patch of the towel over it and applied pressure. The doorbell rang, and I flinched. "Oh, who now?"

"I'll get it. Keep pressing on that." Lukas disappeared down the hall.

I lifted the cloth. The cuts didn't look so bad, I decided. I grabbed a plaster out of the kit and covered the cut to prevent Lukas fussing over my finger any longer.

He appeared in the kitchen entryway and shrugged. "It's your neighbour. She saw the smoke and got worried."

Anna trailed behind him. She kept her head down so that her long hair shielded her face, and kept sneaking wide-eyed glances at Lukas's back. I realised she had to be frightened of strange men—especially tall ones.

I jumped around the bench to offer her some security. "Sorry for worrying you. I fell asleep. Everything's fine now."

"He said your hand—" Anna reached for my arm, but I pulled it back. Blood had already soaked through the plaster. I didn't want her to see.

"Yeah, I cut it. But enough about me. We have some cameras to set up."

"Jo…" Lukas started then hesitated.

Anna glanced at Lukas then shifted a little closer to me. "Cameras?"

"Yeah. Lukas is a film director. He borrowed some motion-sensor stuff. That way, if Raul comes back, you'll have advance warning."

"Oh!" Anna's face lit up. "That's a great idea. It will make it easier to sleep."

"Huh…" Lukas rubbed a hand over the back of his neck, looking surprised.

I glared at him. "What?"

"Nothing." He shrugged. "Just…nothing."

It took a second, then realisation made angry heat rise into my face. "What? You thought I was making it up?"

"Eh…"

"Oh, you absolute jerk."

"Be fair. It was a weird story to begin with, and then I arrived to find you'd nearly burnt your house down. I thought you'd gone batty."

I punched his shoulder, softly enough that I wouldn't hurt him but hard enough that he knew I was serious. "Well, the neighbour's real, the ex is real, and the ghosts are real, too. Go get your cameras."

"Oh yeah, and the ghosts." He rolled his eyes skyward. "I'd nearly forgotten about that delightful angle."

"I saw them."

"Agree to disagree. Weirdo."

I folded my arms as Lukas stomped down the hallway, but a smile curled at the corners of my mouth. He was back to insulting me. That was miles better than the cautious concern.

Anna stood perfectly still by my side, alternating glances between Lukas's retreating back and my face. I shrugged. "Don't mind him. He's crusty around the edges but a marshmallow inside."

"All right." She rubbed her hands over her arms. "But maybe we don't really need the cameras. I don't want to inconvenience him."

"Oh, don't worry. He drove more than an hour to get here. He'll be way more annoyed if we send him away without doing anything. Come on." I ushered her ahead of me towards the front door. As I left, I scanned the kitchen a final time. The burnt cake rested on the stove. The setting sun filled the room with an orange glow. The bitter tang of smoke still hung in the air, but it was gradually filtering out through the open windows. And the doll on the sill, her blue eyes shining, watched me go.

CHAPTER 13

LUKAS OPENED THE BACK doors of his van and began carting boxes of equipment up to Anna's porch. I tried to help, but he insisted he didn't want anyone else touching his stuff. I think he mostly just didn't want to get blood over it.

"All right"—he slammed the van's doors closed—"that's everything. We have four sets of cameras. I'd suggest putting one in the front porch here, facing that direction so that it catches the windows, too. Where did you want the others?"

Anna and I exchanged a look. "One at the back door," she decided. "And, uh…what do you think, Jo?"

"One in the foyer. And one in the upstairs hallway."

Lukas sighed as he turned to Anna. "You don't have to humour her ghost theory, you know."

"N-No, I think those would be good places. I mean, w-we should have some coverage inside the house, just in case—"

"All right, I'll set it up. I'll also need some space to set up a monitoring area. A table about this long." He held out his hands.

"Dining room," Anna said. She was gradually shrinking behind me. "I don't really use it for eating anyway."

"Works for me." Lukas had already taken a camera out of a bag. He brushed a cluster of cobwebs away from the porch's back corner and examined the area. "I'm going to have to drill some holes. You all right with that?"

"Sure. Whatever you need to do."

I nudged Anna's shoulder. "Let's go get something to drink while we wait."

Inside, the house felt cooler than the outdoors, so I kept my jacket on. I couldn't stop myself from scanning the shadows as we moved through the foyer and towards the kitchens. "No problems with the house today?"

"No. It's been lovely and quiet. I had time to package the last set of dolls and get them ready for mailing. I'll start on a new batch this evening, if I have time."

"Good. They're still selling quickly?"

"Within five minutes." She laughed. "If this gets any bigger, I'll have to hire employees."

Anna's kitchen window overlooked the backyard. I couldn't stop myself from staring at the big oak tree at the back of the property. I tried to visualise Ray Marwick hanging from it, his head tilted at an angle, limbs limp, as a rope cinched around his neck.

Had Helen really made him do it, or had he just been plagued by guilt?

"I think I know who the ghost is," I said. "I asked around town. The lady over the street knew the Marwick family."

"Oh, that's good." Anna lifted the teabags out of our cups and carefully added milk. I waited for her to ask for details. She stayed vexingly silent.

"Her name's Helen," I said, more for my own satisfaction than Anna's.

She smiled and passed me my cup. "That's a pretty name. Helen. I like it."

I ran my thumb over the teacup's edge. I didn't fully understand her attitude. If my house were haunted, I would want to know everything I possibly could about it...but then, I wouldn't have bought Marwick House in the first place. Maybe Anna really was more comfortable with this sort of thing than I was.

"You said Lukas was a film director, didn't you?"

"Yeah."

She made a face. "Seems like an awfully important person to be spending their afternoon installing cameras at my house. He must be very fond of you."

I laughed. "Wrong on both counts. He's out of a job right now. This sort of stuff is good for him; a distraction might stop him from being so cranky all the time."

"I heard that," Lukas yelled from the foyer.

"Seriously, though." I watched my reflection in my tea. "Raul was circling around your house for hours last night. I hope this will make things a bit safer."

Anna was quiet. In the background, Lukas's drill roared for a moment then fell silent.

"I saw her in the mirror," Anna said.

I looked up. "What?"

"The ghost. Helen." Anna took a sip of her tea. She didn't expound, and I was forced to ask.

"When? What did she look like?"

"Earlier today. I was brushing my teeth and looked up at my reflection. She stood in the corner of the room, beside the shower curtain. She was watching me."

I wanted to shake her but kept myself firmly in my chair. "Why didn't you call me?"

"Oh, no, it wasn't like that. I don't think she was trying to scare me." Anna looked nervous, apparently afraid I would disagree. "She disappeared as soon as I looked at her. I think she was just…saying hello."

It was a miracle she hadn't screamed. I would have. "She had black hair, didn't she?"

"Yeah."

"And a grey dress."

"Same shade as the bedroom curtains." Anna smiled at her tea. "I know you'll think I'm strange for saying this—and I can recognise how strange it is, too—but it's almost nice to have her here. I feel like she's keeping an eye out for me."

I looked around the room. Anna might not care, but I didn't like being watched. Night had fallen while we'd talked, and I glanced towards the window. A hint of motion drew my attention to the space just beyond the glass. I locked my eyes on it, but there wasn't anything there.

"Well, I hope she's nice, like you think," I said. "Maybe she'll wave to the cameras."

As if on cue, Lukas appeared in the doorway. "I've got that all installed. Now I just need to set up the monitoring system. I'd appreciate some help, if anyone feels up to it." He pointed to me as I stood. "Not you, Jo, your hand's a mess."

"My hand's fine," I grumbled as I followed Anna out of the room.

Lukas explained how the monitoring systems worked while he installed them. He'd run cables to all of the cameras that fed back to the same computer. When the motion sensors tripped, the cameras would turn on and their feed would appear on the computer screen. At the same time, the system would beep to alert us to activity. Lukas had a separate device that looked like a walkie-talkie. He said Anna could take it with her to the bathroom and keep it next to her bed at night so she wouldn't miss the alarm.

"That should be pretty much done." Lukas plugged in the final cable. "We'll just test that they work and—"

The machine beeped, and the screen flashed to life. It showed the upstairs hallway. Lukas stared at it for a moment then frowned. "It shouldn't be doing that unless it caught movement."

Anna had her eyes fixed on the screen and her hands clasped in her lap. Her lips tightened.

The computer beeped again. The hallway remained empty.

"All right, it's obviously malfunctioning." Lukas turned towards the stairway. "I'll see if I can find what the problem is."

Beep. I folded my arms across my chest. Lukas's boots thumped up the stairs, beating at the already-weary planks, then he appeared in the lower corner of the camera's screen. He raised a hand towards the camera, and it beeped.

"Do you see anything?" I called.

"No cobwebs," he yelled back. "No protrusions or drapes that could be shifting. Hang on a moment." He backed up the hallway, watching the camera and moving his arms to check the sensor's range. Something shifted in the upper corner of the screen. I leaned forward and squinted. The camera's frame captured the bottom half of the doorway at the end of the hall. A grey shape moved inside. *The curtains? No...*

Lukas was nearly halfway down the hallway, but he hadn't turned. The door shifted inwards. The grey shape moved again, and my heart flipped. It definitely wasn't curtains. "Lukas!"

"What?" A scowl darkened his face as he continued to search for what had caused the motion sensor to go off. I stood so sharply that my chair fell over. The sallow woman paced down the hallway, advancing on Lukas, a length of chains clenched in her grey hands.

"Lukas, behind you!"

He started to turn. "What are you talking ab—"

A bright flash blinded me. When I blinked my eyes open, the house was almost perfectly dark.

My breathing was a rasping grate in my ears. I felt blindly, and my fingers found the table's edge. "Anna?"

"I'm here." She sounded calm. Almost too much so.

"Don't move." I turned towards the stairs. The curtains were still drawn from when we'd hidden from Raul the night before, and almost no moonlight made it into the house. I found the bannister with my shins, and from there, I fumbled my way onto the steps. "Lukas!"

"I must have tripped the power," he called back. "Hang on."

"Lukas, there was a woman behind you—"

My words were drowned out by a sharp cry. I couldn't breathe. My feet tripped over a stair, and I hit the boards with a heavy thud. "Lukas!"

Marwick House was silent. I scrambled upwards, using all four limbs to gain the hallway. The air tasted bitter—worse than the burning cake—and I choked on it. The house was too dark. I felt forward, searching for Lukas by touch. My eyes were wide but blind, and my fingers grazed only cool air. "Lukas?"

I stretched farther forward, reaching into the shadows. Clammy, cool fingers touched mine.

The sensation was unlike anything I'd experienced before. The skin felt unnaturally spongy and too cold. My first thought was that I'd brushed hands with a corpse. I gasped and recoiled. A whining buzz filled the hallway, and the lights flickered as they came on one at a time.

Lukas crouched against the wall a few paces away from me.

His face was grey and pocked with perspiration, and he clutched a hand over his forearm.

"You okay?" I crawled towards him. The bitter smell had disappeared when the lights came on. I could breathe again.

"What…" His eyes shifted from me to the hallway behind himself. He took his hand away, and I saw three red scores marking his upper arm, like scratches left by fingernails. He stared at them, then his Adam's apple bobbed as he swallowed. "Did you do this?"

"No. There was someone behind you." Wariness grew over his expression, and I rushed on, desperate to make him believe. "It was a woman. Anna saw it, too—ask her!"

A beep echoed from downstairs as the motion detector went off again. Lukas and I stared at each other for a moment, then Lukas spoke, his voice raspy. "We shouldn't leave her alone."

I stood and offered him a hand up, but he didn't take it. Bright blood welled in the cuts on his arm, but at least it wasn't flowing. He rose, not meeting my eyes, and pressed past me to reach the stairwell.

"Ask Anna," I begged. "I'm not lying!"

I jogged to catch up to him and nearly bumped into his back. He'd frozen on the top of the stairs.

From our vantage point, we had a view through the doorway into the dining room. Anna had turned her chair around to face the staircase. She sat, her hands folded neatly in her lap, her head tilted to the side a fraction as though curious to see us. Her long hair seemed to glow in the golden light, and her eyes seemed bigger and bluer than ever.

The woman stood behind the chair, her long, mottled fingers resting on Anna's shoulders. She leaned forward, almost curling around Anna, as grey eyes stared at us from under matted black hair.

Then she was gone.

CHAPTER 14

I TURNED TO LUKAS, nearly frantic with excitement and stress. "You saw that! You saw, didn't you? Say you saw her!"

His lips parted a fraction. His fingers gripped the bannister, and the knuckles turned white from the pressure. "Ah—ah—"

I shook his shoulder. "Lukas?"

He looked at me as though he hadn't realised I was there. His eyes were wide and filled with terror. Then he staggered away from me, stumbling down the remainder of the stairs and knocking the awful watercolours askew.

Anna waited patiently in her chair, watching us, but Lukas didn't go to her. He stumbled into the front door, wrenched it open, and vanished outside.

"Lukas!" I hesitated in the foyer, part of me wanting to keep Anna safe, part afraid that Lukas would run into the street and be hit by a car. Anna gave me a small calm smile, so I followed my cousin outside.

He'd come to a halt at the end of the yard. He bent over, hands braced on his knees, as he was sick in my bushes. I jogged to catch up to him then patted his shoulder helplessly.

"It's all right. You're all right."

He gasped in a breath and straightened, leaning against the fence for support. Perspiration shone over his face. "What part of this is *all right*, Jo?"

"Ehh…" All I could do was shrug. "I'm really sorry."

He wiped the back of his hand over his mouth. For a moment, he did nothing but breathe and lean on the pickets, then he turned his head to squint at me. "Can you tell me this is a joke? Please? Light and mirrors, designed to frighten old sceptic Lukas? Is that why you wanted the cameras—to catch my reaction?"

His tone wasn't accusing, but pleading. He was grasping at anything he could find to keep his footing on his belief—or rather, lack of belief—in the supernatural.

I exhaled and leaned my back against the fence, careful to avoid the place where he'd thrown up. "I wish I could. Really. I'm sorry. But I wanted the cameras because this stuff has been going on for weeks, ever since Anna moved in."

"Okay." He pinched the bridge of his nose and squeezed his eyes closed. "Okay. I'm not going back in there. And you're not, either. Is that thing…attached to Anna?"

"I don't know. I don't think so. I think it stays with the house."

"Okay. Then call Anna. The three of us are getting away from this place."

"Where? I don't want to visit your mother."

"Then we'll stay in a hotel." He straightened. The panic lingered in his eyes, and his shoulders shook, but he seemed to be regaining control over himself. "Somewhere a long way from here."

"Can you afford one? Because I can't, and Anna can't. Not long-term, I mean. And there's no point in leaving for one night if we just have to come back tomorrow."

"Ugh." He began pacing. "Please stop talking sense, Jo. It's disorienting."

I laughed and gave his shoulder another pat. "It's really all right. Like I said, this stuff has been happening for a while. Why don't you crash at my place tonight? I'll make you a bed on the couch."

He continued pacing. At the end of every lap, he paused to look at the house as though it might have an answer for him. I was starting to grow restless by the time he said, "All right."

"Okay. Stay here a moment. I'll go check on Anna."

I left Lukas at the top of the driveway and jogged back to the front door. Anna stood just inside the foyer, waiting for me. She spoke before I caught my breath. "How is he?"

"Coping, I think." I rubbed my hands over my arms as I glanced behind her, into the shadowed house. "Did you see… *her?*"

Anna glanced over her shoulder. "No, but I felt her. Like that prickling sensation you get when someone walks into the room." When she turned back to me, her smile hadn't slipped. She didn't look even half as unsettled as I felt.

"Lukas is staying at my place tonight. Come over, too. We'll order in some Chinese and watch a movie or something."

"Thanks, Jo, that's really kind. But I think I'd like to stay here tonight."

I couldn't keep the incredulity off my face.

She laughed. "Things have been a bit weird for a while, and I feel like I just need some stability. Besides, I've got a new batch of dolls to make. I have some really cute ideas I want to try out. How about we catch up tomorrow instead?"

"Lukas's arm is all scratched up!" I waved a hand behind me, to where my cousin was stubbornly waiting beyond Marwick's boundaries. "And you're just…fine about that?"

Finally, her smile dipped. She clenched her hands together. "I'm really sorry about that. I feel like it was probably an accident—he might have startled Helen or something. She's never shown any tendency to violence before."

"What if you're wrong? What if she's a dangerous spirit? Are you really going to take that chance?"

Her smile fluttered back into life, but it was shaky. "I don't really have much of a choice. It's either this house or a shelter. So, yeah. I want to trust Helen. I want to believe what happened to Lukas was a mistake."

"All right." I exhaled. Anna's smile might have trembled, but her eyes were firm. I could tell I wasn't going to change her mind any time soon, so I backed away from the door. "You've still got my number, right?"

"Yes, it's in my phone."

"Give me a call if there are any problems. And I mean any at all. It doesn't matter how late or how minor. Okay?"

"Thanks, Jo." She was already closing the door. "Have a good sleep."

The lock clicked as the door shut, and I was left staring at the house's stone front. The building looked sleepy with all of its windows closed. I backtracked up the driveway, past the dying grass and the sticks of a long-dead shrub, to Lukas.

"She's not coming." I raised my hands in a helpless shrug at his expression. "She's happy in that house. But she has my number if there are issues."

"Okay." He ran his hand over his jaw as he glared at the building. "Let's get inside. There's a lady over the road who's been watching us, and it's really starting to unnerve me."

Penny was pressed against her window, her unblinking stare fixed on us. I waved to her as we crossed over to my garden. She raised a hand in response but didn't smile.

Duke waited for me inside the house, but as I entered, he hissed and skittered up the stairs. My heart sank as I watched him go. It made me feel like a monster—as though I'd somehow been tainted by the Marwick house and would never be normal again.

"What can I get you?" I injected some energy into my voice as I hung up my jacket. "Tea?"

"Coffee. As strong as you can make it." Lukas's voice had

regained its strength, but he chewed on the corner of his thumb as he stared into the distance. I left him to his thoughts as I went into the kitchen.

The smoke had cleared, so I shut the windows and put the batteries back into the fire alarm. Then I threw the charred remains of my disaster cake into the bin.

As I looked up at the sink, I noticed Anna's doll had tipped onto its side. I set it upright then put the kettle on and began cleaning up the mess. The blood drops had partially dried, and it took several long minutes of scrubbing to get them off the bench and the floor.

When I brought Lukas his coffee, I found him sitting in the lounge room, staring at the house next door. He grunted thanks when I put the cup next to him, but his eyes didn't move from the building.

"What do you want for dinner?"

"Doesn't matter. Anything."

I figured the day had been dramatic enough to justify some splurging, so I called up the nearby Chinese eatery and placed an order for my favourite dishes. It was near their closing time, but the owner agreed to deliver the food on his way home and promised it wouldn't take long. Then I made myself a cup of tea, returned to the sitting room, and took the seat next to Lukas. The lines around his eyes and the thousand-yard-stare told me he still needed time to process his thoughts, so I let him sit in silence.

We could see the front half of the Marwick house through the window. Lights turned on and off again as Anna moved through the building, making her own late dinner then retreating to the back half of the house, probably to work on her dolls.

Lukas chewed on his thumb as he watched her silhouette disappear. "How much do you know about ghosts?"

"Not much," I admitted. "Most of what I have is hearsay." I briefly told him Penny's story about Helen and Ray and mentioned the nightmare I'd had when sleeping over. He lapsed back into silence. The doorbell rang, and I jumped up to collect our food.

The man on the doorstep was scowling when I answered. He handed over my food, accepted payment, then nodded towards the Marwick house. "What's up with that place?"

"What do you mean?"

He gave me an odd look, then shrugged. "I dunno. I felt sick when I drove past it. Is there some kind of gas leak or something?"

I swallowed. "Maybe. I'll mention it to the owner."

He nodded and returned to his motorbike. I closed the door but watched through the curtain as he stared at the house for another long minute before driving off in the opposite direction.

CHAPTER 15

I MADE LUKAS A bed on the couch. He still wasn't talking much, but I noticed he grew restless whenever I left the room for more than a few minutes, so I made my own couch-bed opposite. When I asked if he wanted to watch TV, he said he didn't care, so I flipped through the channels. There wasn't anything good on. I turned off the TV, and we sat in silence, both watching the house next door.

A little after midnight, Marwick's living room light turned on. We watched for a silhouette behind the curtains, but none appeared.

"The light's not going to turn off until Anna gets downstairs tomorrow," I said. "Did you want to move to another room?"

"No, I'm fine here."

"All right."

I lay down and pulled the blankets over my head to block out the light. Lukas stayed sitting. I don't know how long it took him to fall asleep, only that he was still alert by the time I finally drifted off an hour later.

When I woke the next morning, my house was saturated with the smell of coffee. I rolled off the couch and shambled into the kitchen, where Lukas was chewing on toast and clutching a cup of coffee that I suspected was not his first.

"Morning," I said, dropping into the chair opposite him. "Make yourself at home, by the way."

He looked wholly different that morning. The awful dazed look had left his eyes, and his face had animation back in it. He'd showered and shaved, too, and plasters covered the scratches on his arm. Instead of responding to my lazy jab, he said, "I want to know more about that house."

"Oh. Okay."

He dropped the toast back onto his plate and took a gulp of the black coffee. "I want to talk to Anna. I want to watch the videos. I need to *understand*."

"I mean, as long as Anna agrees, sure." I scratched at my scalp. I hoped it was a good sign that Anna hadn't called during the night. "She's got a lot going on right now."

"Of course." He hunkered farther over the bench. "But this—I've never seen anything like this before. I've been thinking about it all night. I'm not delusional. I'm not paranoid. But last night, I saw a woman who doesn't exist, and I can't explain it, but I need to."

"I can explain it." I was still sleepy, and that bled into vague irritability. "Ghosts."

"Yes. As you've been saying all along. And maybe that's the conclusion I need to accept. Or maybe there's another solution. That's what I need to find out." He drained his coffee and put the cup back on the bench with a crisp clack. "Do you want to come?"

"What? Of course." I was a little insulted that he would even consider leaving me behind.

"Great. Get changed. The Marwick house's downstairs light turned off half an hour ago, which means Anna's probably awake."

Lukas's sudden burst of energy was a good change, but I still grumbled as I staggered upstairs. I took the world's quickest shower and threw on the first clean clothes I could find, but Lukas was already tapping his foot impatiently by the time I met him at the base of the stairs.

The sky was overcast, making the world look colder than it actually was. We took the familiar path to the front of my property, around the fence, and into Marwick's. I felt eyes on my back and knew Penny still lurked at her window seat, but that didn't bother me. Whatever she might be imagining was nothing compared to what we'd actually experienced.

Anna looked happy when she answered the door. She wore an old T-shirt with paint stains over it, but her hair was neat. I guessed she looked a whole lot fresher than I did. She invited us inside then hesitated in the foyer.

"I'm sorry about last night, Lukas. I hope you weren't startled too badly."

"That's why I'm here, actually." He clasped his hands behind his back. "I want to understand what's happening in this house. Do you mind if I take a look at the security system?"

She shrugged. "Of course. Can I get you something to drink?"

"Coffee would be great, if you have it. Thanks."

I narrowed my eyes at him. *How come he's never that polite to me?*

Lukas went straight to the computer in the dining room. I followed and watched as he fiddled with the switches and cables for a moment. Then he stood back and ran his hands through his hair. "They were unplugged."

"Yes, sorry, that was me." Anna appeared behind us, carrying two cups of coffee. "It wouldn't stop beeping, so I turned it off. I'm really sorry."

"Hm." Lukas's eyes lingered on Anna for a moment then skipped over the room. I wondered if, like me, he was looking for the dark-haired woman. "Okay if I plug it back in?"

"Sure. Is it okay if I leave you to it? I've got some work to do upstairs."

"Go for it. I might be a while here." Lukas settled into the desk and plugged in a cable. Almost immediately, the computer beeped, and the upstairs video turned on. We watched the empty hallway, both searching for any form of movement in the shadows, then jumped as the computer beeped again. Anna appeared in the bottom of the screen, walking towards the room at the end of the hallway.

I almost wanted to call her back down—to tell her not to go

into the blue room where Helen lurked—but she'd seen the same footage I had. She knew exactly what lingered up there. And it didn't frighten her.

The screen went dead after thirty seconds of no movement. Then we had another ping, and the camera at the back door lit up. Again, Lukas and I hunted for movement—and found no results. Another ping, and we were back at the upstairs hallway. I settled into a chair at his side. We watched the screen for four hours. Every one of the house's four cameras lit up multiple times, with most of the activity in the upstairs hallway.

By the time midday rolled around, my neck was stiff and my eyes ached. I knew we weren't going to see anything on the cameras. Lukas seemed to think so, as well, because he stretched and stood. "I'm going to run into town to get us some lunch. What does Anna like?"

"I'm not sure, actually."

"I'll get a couple of different things, then. See you in twenty."

I stayed by the computer while Lukas left. The foyer and front porch's cameras pinged as he passed them, then there was another ping from the upstairs hallway. I exhaled a groan. Maybe the cameras really were faulty, and it was just coincidence that the house was also haunted.

A soft note floated from the piano room. I twisted towards it, holding my breath, then stood as another note followed. The warped, miserable melody built, one note tumbling onto another, escalating, reeling me in like an invisible hook. I moved towards the room. The door was nearly closed; only a sliver of light came through the crack. If I moved to get the angle just right, I could swear I saw motion inside the room. Slate-blue dress. Black hair. Pale skin moving rhythmically as she plucked at the piano keys.

I pressed the door open. The apparition was gone. The song's final, mournful notes hung in the air like whispers.

"Helen?" I hesitated in the doorway, not sure what to do or what to say, only that I wanted to communicate with the spirit. "Helen, I'm sorry for interrupting your song—"

A cold wind ghosted over the back of my neck. I pressed my hand to it and turned. The room seemed unusually quiet. I rotated in a circle, scanning the long drapes, paintings, and mirrors hung about the space.

A soft *click, click, click* made me swivel. It sounded like women's shoes on a hardwood floor. I felt eyes on me. My skin rose into goose bumps, and my heart missed a beat. A large gold-framed mirror hung on the wall behind me. Helen stared at me through the age-fogged glass.

My mouth was too dry to make any sort of noise. I stared at the wraith, and she stared back, her eyes cold and angry behind the matt of black hair. Her cracked lips parted to mouth a word: *Leave.*

Then the front door slammed, and the vision was gone. I gasped in a shaking breath.

Lukas's heavy shoes stomped through the foyer and into the dining room. "Jo?"

"She was here." I backed out of the music room, my eyes still fixed on the mirror, and pointed through the open door. "Helen was here. Playing the piano."

Lukas rested against the table's edge. I could see the internal war in his eyes. The rational part of his mind wanted to dismiss my story, but the practical side was trying to be accepting. "Okay." He spoke slowly. "Do you recognise the song?"

"No, only that it's a sad one. Somewhere between a lullaby and a dirge. It's the song I heard in the dream." I wrapped my arms around my shivering torso. "Then when I entered the room, she appeared in the mirror. She said, 'Leave.'"

"Why would she want you to leave?"

We both turned at Anna's voice. She stood at base of the stairs, her hand resting on the bannister, her blue eyes wide. "Did you do something to upset her?"

"No! I mean, I don't think so…"

Anna chewed on her lip. No one spoke for a moment, then Lukas broke the silence with, "I brought lunch. How about we eat it outside?"

The backyard, despite the dead plants and the still-fresh mound of dirt in the back corner, was a welcome break from the house's stuffy interior. Lukas had brought salads, sandwiches, hot chips, and fresh fruit. He laid it out across the back step, and we helped ourselves. To my surprise, Anna and Lukas struck up a conversation. He wanted to know more about her experiences in the house, and she seemed happy to recount them. I didn't mind. I was happy to let my mind wander.

My finger ached. I picked at the corner of the plaster. Taking it off would only make the pain worse, but I hated not seeing what it looked like. What if the splinter was still in there?

"Jo?" Lukas broke through my thoughts by prodding my shoulder. "Jo, did you hear that?"

"Sorry, what?"

"Anna and I are thinking about calling a spirit medium."

I stared at him. The idea that Sceptical Luke wanted to call a ghost hunter was almost laughable, and I half-wondered if he was joking. But Anna sat on his other side, nodding and smiling, apparently no longer frightened of my tall, caustic cousin.

"That sounds like a plan." I dusted my hands. "Got any contacts?"

He laughed. "As if. But I'll see if I can find someone local. Maybe they'll be able to tell us a bit more about what we're dealing with."

I nodded slowly. It made sense. Maybe someone with experience could remove—or at least pacify—Helen Marwick.

CHAPTER 16

THE THREE OF US banded together around the computer to search for a spirit medium. Lukas automatically rejected anyone who seemed to do it as a hobby or didn't take it seriously enough for his liking, which restricted our options considerably. Turned out very few people conducted séances as their full-time job.

We eventually settled on an older man named Henry Lobbs. He lived a few towns away but was willing to travel. Anna was initially reluctant to invite a man into her home, but Henry had a photo on his site. His mop of wild grey hair and slightly-too-large cardigan gave him the air of a doting grandfather, which softened Anna. She agreed to have him visit as long as Lukas and I were there. Not that we would have had it any other way.

Henry's earliest appointment time was two days later, on a Monday, so we settled in for a weekend of waiting. Lukas stayed with me instead of returning home, which I didn't mind. I liked having company. Not that I got much of it; he spent more than half of his time in the Marwick house. He claimed to be watching the cameras, but several times, I heard laughter floating out of the house next door. Once, when I was hanging out my washing, I saw Lukas and Anna walking through her backyard. They had their heads inclined towards each other as they talked. It would have been almost picturesque if the ground had any colour and the plants weren't all dead.

I spent a few hours with either Lukas or Anna in the Marwick house each day and filled in my spare time with baking. It was the only thing that kept my mind quiet. I specifically stuck to recipes I was familiar with and managed to avoid starting any more fires.

Monday seemed to take an eternity to roll around. Henry wasn't due to arrive until noon, but both Lukas and I went to the Marwick house early. Lukas ducked into the dining room to check on the cameras while Anna and I prepared some sand-wiches for lunch.

"Are you excited?" I asked.

She shrugged. "More nervous. What if he makes it worse?"

"He'd better not." I snorted. "Not if he wants his bill paid."

Anna laughed. She seemed to be in a good mood, and I thought I could guess why. "How're the dolls going?"

"Great! I just finished this new batch last night. They're really cute! I tried a few new styles, and I think people will like them." She bit her lip. "Can I ask a stupid question?"

"It can't be any stupider than mine. Go ahead."

"Would Lukas like a doll? I mean—would he think I'm weird if I gave him one?"

I narrowed my eyes at Anna. "You've become very buddy-buddy with him, haven't you?"

Bright-pink colour spread over her cheeks and ears. She wouldn't meet my eyes. "No! I mean, he's been so generous with his time—and I wanted to give him something to thank him—but I don't really have anything to offer except the dolls…"

I nudged her with my elbow. "He's not really a doll guy, but coming from you, I bet he'd like it."

"Hey." Lukas knocked on the kitchen doorframe.

Anna twitched and turned an even brighter shade of pink.

I stacked a sandwich onto the platter we were preparing and wiped my hands on a cloth. "What's up?"

"One of the cameras is broken. You didn't hear anything last night, did you, Anna?"

Her eyes widened. "No—but I keep the volume off at night. They ping constantly otherwise. I'm really sorry. Which one broke?"

"The one on the veranda. It looks like someone threw a rock at it."

Anna and I exchanged a glance. We hurried past Lukas and out to the front of the house to examine the damage.

The camera was still attached to the wall with a metal bracket, but its front lens had been smashed. I scanned the veranda and found a large, jagged rock lying near the stairs. "What do we think? Was this human?"

Lukas folded his arms and lifted his shoulders in a shrug. "That's my bet. It was fine yesterday afternoon."

"I don't watch the streets much." Anna shot me a pleading look. "You haven't seen Raul's car recently, have you?"

"No...but I haven't been watching the street much, either." I ran my hands through my hair. "Penny across the road sometimes sits at her window at night. You guys stay here and wait for our spirit medium. I'll run over and ask her."

Anna and Lukas returned indoors while I jogged across the road. Unlike previous visits, Penny didn't open the door on my first knock. I had to beat my fist against the door for nearly a minute before I heard her footsteps echoing down the hallway. She unlocked the door but only opened it a crack. I had to lean against the house's side to meet the single beady eye watching me through the opening.

"Hey, Penny, is this a bad time?"

"It is." Her voice was curt. "I'd prefer not to talk today."

"Oh." Shock muted me for a moment. I'd never known Penny to pass up a chance for gossip before. "Sorry—I just had one question. Have you seen a red sports car driving down this street recently? Specifically, last night?"

"No." She began to close the door.

I put my hand out to stop it from being shut in my face and lowered my voice. "Penny, is something wrong? Did I...do something to upset you?"

"No." Her tone was still frosty but a little less curt. She hesitated. "It's not you; it's the house. There's something not right about that building. I don't watch it anymore. And I recommend you stay away from it, too."

"I…" I glanced behind myself. The Marwick house looked no more sinister than normal. Its vine-choked stone walls, its blurred, curtained sash windows, and its uneven shingled roof were grim, but they left me feeling more fascinated than repulsed. "What's wrong with it?"

Penny's beady eye scanned my face. She seemed reluctant to answer. "I don't know. But I can tell you I want no part in it. You're a smart girl, Jo. Put some distance between yourself and that building before it ensnares you, too." She paused for a moment then added, "I haven't seen a sports car. But that doesn't mean much. I haven't watched the street these last few days. Goodbye."

I stepped back as the door slammed. I tried not to take Penny's words personally, but it still hurt. After Anna, Penny was the closest thing I had to a friend in our street.

There's no staying away now, I thought as I stalked across the road and stepped back onto the dead lawn. *I've already gone too far. I can't just ignore Anna or her house, like Penny is. I can't pretend they don't exist.*

Lukas was on the porch, taking the camera out of its bracket. "Any luck?"

"No. She hasn't been watching the street."

He raised an eyebrow at me. "Isn't she meant to be the town gossip or something? Has she been sick?"

"In a way." I didn't want to elaborate, and Lukas didn't press.

He returned to his bolts while I made my way back to the kitchen. A soft humming tune echoed through the house. I paused in the foyer as I recognised it: it was the same lilting, mournful lullaby that continued to haunt me.

Anna stepped out of the kitchen, carrying the tray of sandwiches…and humming the tune.

"All done?" I asked, mostly just to get her to stop.

"Yep. I cleaned up, as well, so we can relax while we wait for this ghost medium." She carried the sandwiches into the dining room and left the tray next to the surveillance equipment. We'd all grown tired of the incessant beeps and had silenced the machine the previous day, but the screen kept changing, flicking between the upstairs hallway, the foyer, and the backyard.

I stopped and stared at the screen. The view of the backyard had changed. Something large hung from the tree at the back. I leaned forward, trying to make out the shape through the grainy distortion, but then the image changed to the upstairs hallway.

"What is it?" Anna asked. I raised a hand to ask her to wait. The screen focused on the hall for a moment then returned to the backyard. The shape hanging from the tree rotated slowly.

"There's something in the yard." I turned away from the screen and jogged through the house. Anna followed. I burst through the back door, my heart pounding, and stared at the tree above the animal grave. There was nothing there.

I swallowed a lump in my throat and carefully descended the steps into the garden. I could visualise the exact place the shape had hung from. I approached the tree, my palms sweaty and my skin prickling, and stared up at the limb.

Rope burns dug into the dark wood. They'd scored a line through the bark, leaving it raw and ragged. I had to stand on my toes to touch them. They felt cool—even cooler than the frosty winter air.

"Jo?" Anna had stopped at the house's back door. She leaned on the frame, concern pulling her eyebrows together. "I can hear Lukas talking to someone. I think the spirit medium has arrived."

"All right." I let my fingers linger on the damaged wood for a second then stepped away. I couldn't suppress a shudder as I turned back to Marwick House.

CHAPTER 17

WE'D MADE A GOOD choice with Henry Lobbs, I decided as I shook his hand. He was perfectly on time, dressed professionally, and carried a briefcase, which Lukas approved of, but he was short and tripped over his words. The man was about as unthreatening as a human could get, which helped Anna. He seemed excited about the job, too, which was a good sign. He asked to discuss our experiences before beginning work.

We gathered around the side of the dinner table that wasn't cluttered with computer equipment. Henry took out a notepad and pen.

"Please don't think I don't believe you," he said, pushing his thick-rimmed glasses farther up his nose. "But oftentimes, seemingly supernatural events have perfectly natural causes. I try to rule them out first off so that I don't waste your time."

Lukas raised a hand. "I never believed in this kind of stuff, but then I saw it with my own eyes. I'd be thrilled if you found an alternate explanation, but I really don't think you will."

"No, well…we'll try, at least." Henry shuffled his papers. "Start at the beginning, and tell me everything you can remember."

We took turns recounting our experiences in the house while Henry jotted down notes. He became very interested when we got to seeing the woman on the cameras. "Were you able to record it?"

"Unfortunately not." Lukas nodded towards the screens. "I didn't have the recorder enabled for the first encounter, then, once it was working, the constant motion triggers burnt through its memory within an hour."

"That's a shame. Keep going, please."

I mentioned the feeling of foreboding I felt when stepping onto the property, the way my cats would avoid it, and how even visitors commented on its atmosphere. Henry seemed very interested when he heard that the deliveryman had mentioned a gas leak.

"That's a possible cause. A leak can cause hallucinations and feelings of paranoia, without being noticeable to residents. I brought a reader, so I'll check through the rooms to see if I find anything."

"And, um…" Anna sat as far away from Henry as she could be but leaned forward to ask her question. "What if it is a ghost? What do we do then?"

"That's up to you, miss. I can try to make contact with the spirit to discern its motives and intentions. Oftentimes, it's possible to clear ghosts, or convince them to move on, with a few simple procedures. Or, if we decide the spirit isn't malevolent, you may be happy to let it continue living in your home."

I thought of the murderous glare Helen had given me through the mirror. Anna believed the ghost was friendly, and I dearly wanted her to be right, but I struggled to believe it.

"First, we'll have a look around, see what I can sense, and rule out a couple of natural causes." Henry unlocked his briefcase. He'd brought a handful of small contraptions, and took two out. "This is a gas reader"—he held up the first one—"and this records infrasound pulses. Like gas, sometimes infrasound can play tricks on our minds. Shall we have a poke around?"

We gave him a tour of the house. Henry paused in each room to read the machines' numbers and note them down. "So far, we're not getting any response from the gas reader, which is a good sign. You don't want to be living in a house with a leak."

We looped through the downstairs rooms then made our way up the groaning stairs. Henry paused on the landing and made a low humming noise in the back of his throat.

"What is it?" Lukas asked.

Henry ran a finger around his collar. "Ah…I'm not fully sure. Give me a moment."

His pace slowed as he moved along the hallway. For the first few rooms, he held the readers out ahead of himself, but he gradually lowered them as he progressed. I knew what had attracted his attention before he even reached it.

Henry pressed his hand against the door at the end of the hall and stepped into the blue room. He stared around the space, his eyes vacant and his jaw slack. Anna stepped closer to me, and I put my arm around her shoulder for comfort.

"She was here…" Henry's voice had taken on a strange lilt. He reached out a hand and pointed shaking fingers towards the wall. "That's where he chained her. Bolts in the wall. It took her a long time to pull them out."

My stomach flipped. I looked towards the patch of blue wallpaper where Henry pointed to. There were two tiny dark holes in the paper near the floor.

"She didn't want him to take something…" Henry's breathing increased. He turned away from the wall and looked at the window. "Something precious. Something she loved, that he would have broken. So she leapt. It was better to lose herself…to lose what she loved…than to give it to him."

Henry turned towards us. His face was blanched white and covered in perspiration. When he spoke, his voice was raw and shaking. "I need to get out of this room."

"Okay." Lukas took Henry's shoulder and guided him back to the door.

Anna and I moved aside to make way for them, pressing our backs to the dark-red wood cladding to make room in the narrow space. We exchanged a look before following the men downstairs.

So Ray kept Helen a prisoner. And so she took her own life. But what was the precious thing Henry was talking about? Her sanity, maybe? Her free will?

I stopped at the end of the hallway. I'd felt eyes on the back of my head. I turned back to the blue room, just in time to see the door groan closed.

Lukas took Henry downstairs to the kitchen, where the older man bent over the sink, breathing heavily and splashing water over his face. He took a few minutes to turn around, but when he did, his face had recovered some of its colour.

"Sorry about that." He dried his glasses on a little cloth from his pocket. His smile was shaky. "I don't often get impressions in that way. My grandmother was better at it. Sometimes, she could walk into a room and instantly know what had happened in there. For me…they just come out of the blue sometimes and hit me like a freight train."

"That must have been Helen," I said. "She fell to her death from that window. Her husband buried her in the backyard, but then he hung himself a few months later. Some people think Helen haunted him to his death."

"The vengeful bride. It's a common trope." Henry carefully replaced his glasses. "Do you know the place she was buried?"

"We're not a hundred percent sure, but we have a pretty good guess."

We led Henry into the back garden. Thick low-lying clouds dampened the sun, and a cold breeze wormed its way under my jacket, making me shiver. We stopped under the old tree at the back of the house, and I pointed towards the clump of slightly raised dirt. "That's where we found all of the animal bones."

Henry closed his eyes, and his bushy brows pulled closer together. "Yes…yes, I can feel something here. Just a moment, please."

He circled the space, one hand held towards the ground, his lips tightening into a line. Then he abruptly staggered back, his hands clamped to his stomach as though he'd been punched.

"Henry?" Lukas started towards him, but the spirit medium held up one hand. He doubled over and retched, but nothing came up.

"Do you want to go back inside?" I asked.

He nodded. Lukas put an arm under Henry's left side while I took the right, and we half-carried him towards the house.

We ended up back in the kitchen, with Henry leaned over the sink a second time. Anna, looking anxious, fidgeted with the hem of her blouse. Lukas leaned against the wall, his arms crossed over his chest and his lips scrunched together.

"Well...that was certainly something." Henry straightened, his face flushed and wet. "I think we can safely say that yes, this house does have a resident spirit, and yes, she's not particularly fond of my presence."

"What happened out there?" I asked.

"I tried to make contact with her. Sometimes, spirits will communicate with me—they'll tell me what they want or why they're on earth or ask for help passing over. She didn't want any of that, though. I felt a strong repulsion towards me. Well, more towards what I represent. She hates men."

"Understandable if her husband chained her up," Anna muttered.

"I've been here for a couple of days now," Lukas said. "I got a couple of light scratches on my arm my first night here, but that's it. She hasn't done anything else to me."

"No, because you're highly resistant." Henry patted his face dry with a towel I'd passed to him. "Spirits find it easier to influence people who are open to them—that is, people who believe in ghosts. You don't. Not fully. You say you do, because right now you have no alternative, but deep down, you're just waiting for a scientific explanation that will dispel all of this supernatural nonsense."

Lukas lifted his eyebrows. "Huh. Maybe you should've been a psychologist instead."

"Oh, I'm not that good. I can just pick your type a mile off." Henry chuckled. "You're every sceptical husband I've ever met. Going along with the cleansing because the wife's in a panic, but secretly thinking there must be a proper reason for why they saw a pen float." Henry indicated to a chair. "May I?"

Anna quickly nodded.

The spirit medium sighed as he sank into the seat. "So, yes, your natural scepticism acts like armour...for now. The longer you stay here, the less effective it will be. But let's not talk about that. We have to make a choice about what to do with your spirit."

The three of us sank into the other seats around the kitchen table.

Henry stared at his hands for a moment before speaking. "Generally, there are four ways to respond to a ghost. The first and easiest is to just ignore it. Most hauntings are mild in nature—perhaps you feel a chill when you walk into a room or get a sensation of being watched. Many families in that situation are happy to leave the spirit as is, and they often forget it's even there after a while. We could try that, though I believe your particular spirit, Helen, is a bit too aggressive to easily ignore."

I propped my chin up in my hands. "What're the other options?"

"The second is to comfort a spirit and encourage it to move on to the next life. That only really works when a ghost is ready to leave, but lingering doubt or fear is holding it to earth. That won't work for us. I felt no fear in your spirit, only anger and resentment. The third method is to close the loop."

"Sorry." Lukas held up a hand. "Could you please explain for the normal people in the room?"

I kicked his leg under the table.

Henry didn't seem to notice the jibe. "A loop is a significant moment tied to a spirit's death. They replay it incessantly— hence the term *loop*. It goes around and around without ever ending. An example might be a murder victim running through her home to relive the seconds before the intruder stabbed her. Or a ghost crossing a street but vanishing halfway, where they were hit by a car in life. If you know the ghost's loop, it's occasionally possible to break it. An example might be driving a car towards the ghost crossing the road, but braking before you hit it. It changes the moment the spirit is reliving…and because they use that moment as an anchor to earth, they lose their tether and simply move on. Do you know Helen's loop, my dear?"

"I…uh—" Anna, flustered, looked to me.

I cleared my throat. "Anna's only been in the house for a

couple of weeks. I mean, I can guess her loop probably has to do with leaping from the window, but we've never actually seen it."

"Some ghosts relive their loop daily. Others may only experience it once a decade." Henry shrugged. "If Helen doesn't like to relive her loop often, there's not much we can do to break it. That brings me to my final solution: a cleansing."

"Yeah, this house needs a cleansing. Have you seen the dust?"

I kicked Lukas's leg a little harder. He grunted and shuffled his chair away from me.

"A spiritual cleansing." Henry spoke patiently, even though I was sure Lukas knew what he'd meant. "It's where we attempt to forcefully expel the ghost from the house. We use smudging—that is, burning sage—and scatter salt. It's not always successful, but it works often enough to be useful."

The three of us turned to Anna.

She blanched under our attention. "W-What should I do?"

"It's your house, miss, and your choice." Henry shrugged. "If you think you can live with the spirit the way she is, we can leave her be. Maybe you'll eventually witness her loop and be able to break it. But if the presence is too threatening, I have equipment for a cleansing in my briefcase. We can perform it right now."

Anna sent a panicked glance towards me.

I leaned closer to her. "What do you want to do?"

"I don't know! What do you think?"

I phrased myself as carefully as I could. "I know you're not bothered by living with a ghost. But I don't think Helen is as friendly as you want her to be. And I'm worried about you living alone with her."

"So…"

"I'd try the cleansing, yeah."

"All right." She swallowed and nodded to Henry. "We'll do that last one. The cleansing. Please."

"Of course." Henry rose with a bright smile. "Let's get started."

CHAPTER 18

HENRY TOOK US BACK to the dining room, where his case rested next to the computers. He unlocked and opened it and took out two bunches of herbs and a large opaque plastic bottle.

"Salt," he explained as he shook the bottle. The grains rustled inside. "It's historically used to purify and clean areas where bad events have happened. And the sage"—he held up the herbs—"is burnt to force spirits to move on. They don't enjoy the scent." He tucked the items into his cardigan's pockets then nodded towards the living room. "If you'd all be so kind to open the windows and doors. It helps to give spirits clear passage outside."

We obediently spread through the house. I tackled the kitchen and laundry windows. Lukas passed me in the hall, and I distinctly heard him mumble something about letting bugs in.

I caught up with Anna on the second floor. She was going

through the bedrooms, squeezing around the aged, faded furniture, and opening their windows. I saw the worry lingering over her face. "Hey, are you all right with this?"

"Hm? Yeah. It's the right thing to do. Isn't it?" She hesitated with her hands resting on an open sill and shivered. "I just…"

"Go on."

"I know it's stupid, but it feels like we're being cruel by forcing her out. This was her house before it was mine."

"I know how you feel." I looked over the outdated furniture and wondered how often Helen must have sat in them. "But she needs to let go of the past. You own this house now. I don't see her paying the rent."

Anna chuckled. She stepped back from the window and folded her arms around herself. "She had a really hard life. I don't want to do anything worse to her."

"Maybe this is a good thing." I shrugged. "If she's been resentful and unhappy the entire time she's been on earth. Maybe it's best for her to move on. Maybe the next life has something nicer waiting for her. Some sort of reward for her suffering."

"Yeah."

We stood staring at the old furniture for a moment, then Anna sighed. "I really hope that's the truth."

We finished opening the windows and retraced our steps downstairs. Lukas and Henry were waiting in the foyer.

Henry gave us a smile. "All ready?"

"Yes, whenever you are."

Henry took out a box of matches and lit the tip of one of the herb bunches. The leaves caught and began to smoulder, sending up wisps of fragrant smoke.

Anna pressed her hand over her nose. "It smells weird."

"The spirits think so, too," Henry said good-naturedly. "Let's begin."

He moved through the rooms slowly, spreading the smoke through the area before scattering salt around the doors and windowsills. As he walked, he spoke in a low, even voice. "You are no longer welcome in this house. It is time to move on. You are no longer welcome in this house."

We passed from the foyer and into the living room. The lights flickered. We all glanced up at the bulb as it stabilised. Henry didn't stop his chant but spread extra smoke around the lights.

Anna hung close to my side as we followed Henry into the dining room. Lukas kept pace not far behind us. I could almost feel the concern emanating from him, and I wondered if our spirit medium had underestimated my cousin's belief.

"It's time to move on. You are not welcome here." Henry scattered salt crystals across the windowpanes as he circled the table. A single low, thrumming note came from the music room. I closed my eyes, waiting for the song to start, but it didn't.

Henry stepped around the table to nudge open the music room door. Its lights were out. He flicked the switch, but they stayed dead. "You are not welcome here."

He was a braver person than me, I decided as Henry stepped into the darkness. The three of us exchanged a glance before following. Prickles crept over my arms as I entered the music room. It almost felt like walking through spiderwebs. My reflexes kicked in, and I rubbed my hands over my skin.

Henry turned slowly. His bushy eyebrows were pulled low, and perspiration dotted his face. "She liked this room. She used to play for hours." He raised his voice. "Helen, it's time to move on."

The curtains curled outwards in the wind. For a second, I imagined I'd seen a silhouette behind them, but then it was gone.

Metal clinked somewhere upstairs. Anna squeezed my arm. Henry lifted his herbs to spread their smoke around the room. A gust of wind blew across the leaves. The sage crumbled. It turned to powder in Henry's hands, the dust falling across the carpet.

"What…" Henry glanced up. The sweat was more noticeable. He ran his finger around his collar. "That shouldn't happen. Shouldn't be possible."

The chains were moving closer to the stairs. When I closed my eyes, I could visualise them: heavy links dragged along the ground by the black-haired woman with pallid skin and staring eyes.

"I have another bunch." Henry backed towards the dining room doorway. "Won't take a minute."

A high-pitched electrical whine buzzed through the house. All of the lights went out. I could still see thanks to the daylight coming through the windows, but the change in the atmosphere was palpable. The shadows gathered more deeply, obscuring the room's corners and clinging to the furniture.

With a sharp clink, the chain was pulled taut. Henry stopped in the doorway, eyes turned towards the ceiling, as we held our breath and listened. The cobweb-like prickles intensified. Then Henry gasped and doubled over. He retched then dropped to his knees with a whine. I ran to him, Lukas close behind me.

"Hey, you okay?" I put a hand on his shoulder.

He was ice cold. Sweat soaked through his shirt. I looked up at Lukas. He was breathing heavily, his face pale.

"Out," Henry gasped. "Get me *out*."

"Okay. Lean on me." I hooked his arm around my shoulder as Lukas lifted from his other side. The three of us staggered down the hallway.

A long, high-pitched note hung in the air. I shot a glance towards the piano, but Anna wasn't anywhere near it. The note lasted far longer than I thought it could have, and it grew louder instead of dulling. It shook inside my skull, making me nauseous and filling me with inexplicable dread.

The front door drifted open as we neared it. The motion made me want to recoil, but Henry was bent on getting outside. I supported him, half guiding and half carrying, as we made our way down the porch and across the dead grass.

I looked behind myself, but Anna wasn't following us. A spike of panic hit me, but then my friend emerged from the house's shadows. Anna jogged after us, carrying Henry's case.

Henry looked a little better once we got him past the edge of the property. He leaned on the fence, gasping in harsh breaths, sweat drenching him. I didn't know what to do, so I hovered beside Anna while we waited for the older man to recover.

He eventually stood straight. His glasses had fogged up, so he took them off to clean them while he caught his breath. "Well. She certainly doesn't like men. You felt it, too, didn't you, Lukas?"

My cousin leaned against the fence. The awful shade of grey had left his face, but he still looked pale. "I felt sick."

"Yes, that's what she can do to you. It will get worse if you stay here longer." Henry took a deep breath, blew it out, then turned to Anna. "I'm going to be honest with you. The cleansing wasn't working. And I don't think I can continue business in your house any longer. In my professional opinion, the ghost is highly volatile, and engaging it further will only exacerbate the problem."

Anna rubbed at her forearms. "What does that mean?"

"I don't believe any ghost is evil, any more than a human has the capacity for both good and bad. But a great deal of bitterness went into shaping Helen Marwick's spirit. I felt resentment, regret, and a lot of anger. As you saw, she is especially mistrustful towards men. If I try to cleanse her from this house again, she will fight back. I believe it would be a dangerous—and potentially counterproductive—measure." He replaced his glasses and tugged at his sweat-soaked collar. "My advice, at this time, would be to give her as little attention as possible. She is feeding off your energy and your fear. It is likely that her manifestations will lessen, and perhaps even cease entirely, if you don't react to them."

Lukas and I glanced at each other. We were the responsible parties for a lot of the recent attention directed towards Helen.

"Don't try to communicate with her," Henry continued. "Don't look for her. Don't react if she shows herself. I believe that will be your safest course of action. Eventually, she may subside into a passive, unnoticeable spirit. At that point, we can consider trying to cleanse the house again. But I wouldn't want to do so before."

"Okay." Anna didn't look anywhere near as disturbed as I felt. "We'll take the cameras down. Will that help?"

"Yes, do that immediately. And if you'll excuse me, I think I'd prefer to put some distance between myself and this building." He chuckled weakly, still leaning against the fence. "I'm sorry I couldn't help more. I'll bill you for a consultation only."

Anna held out the suitcase. "The salt and herbs are still inside. I'll go and get them."

"Don't worry about it. I have plenty more back at the office. Have a good day, and good luck." Henry took his briefcase from Anna.

We all watched as he got into his car, started the engine, and drove away in a screech of tyres. The urgency of his departure reminded me of the previous family fleeing in the middle of the night. It wasn't an encouraging parallel.

I hoped his advice to ignore the spirit would help. I was frightened of what would happen if it didn't.

CHAPTER 19

I HELPED LUKAS DISASSEMBLE the cameras and monitoring setup. He seemed subdued, and I couldn't get any responses out of him beyond monosyllables. He put the broken camera in a separate box to see if it could be repaired and loaded everything into his van. When he closed the door, I said, "It's getting late. Did you want to crash at my place again?"

"Thanks." He slapped my shoulder on the way past. "But I think it's time for me to get home. My mum's been texting me incessantly; she's getting worried."

"Sure."

Lukas retraced his steps to the house's front door, where Anna waited. He thrust his hands into his pockets and rolled his feet. "Thanks for letting me turn your house into a science experiment these last few days. And I'm sorry if anything I've done has made it worse."

She shrugged, her fingers playing with the hem of her cardigan. "It was nice to have you here. And thanks for helping. Did you want to stay for dinner?"

He glanced towards the horizon, where the sun was steadily dropping. "Nah. It's a long drive back. I'd better start early."

"All right. I hope I'll get to see you again soon."

"Sure. I call in on Jo every few months. We can get together for lunch or something." He backed down the steps then raised a hand in farewell. "Take care, Anna. Later, Jo."

I sidled up to stand next to Anna and watched Lukas as he got into the van. "He doesn't tell *me* to take care. He probably wouldn't mind if I tripped down the stairs and broke my neck."

Anna's laugh sounded forced. She ran her hand across the doorframe as her lips tightened again. "I didn't get to give him his doll."

"He'll be back. Eventually. Give it to him then."

"Yeah." She began backing into the house. "Thanks for looking out for me, Jo. I think I'd like some alone time, if it's okay with you."

"Of course. Give me a call if there are any issues."

She glanced into the house then smiled. The expression seemed strangely bitter. "The windows are all closed."

"What?"

"It must have happened some time after getting Mr. Lobbs outside. The windows closed themselves. I guess Helen didn't like them being open. But at least the lights are on again."

I chewed on my lip. "Hey, did you want me to stay for a bit? Some weird stuff has happened today. Maybe it's not a good idea to be alone."

"No, that's all right. I think *alone* is exactly what I need right now. And, like Mr. Lobbs said, it's probably better not to acknowledge her too much."

"Sure." I gave a reluctant sigh. "But keep the phone close. Just in case."

She waved goodbye and shut the door. A second later, an upstairs light turned on. I rubbed at my arms and hoped Anna would find it and turn it off before bedtime.

My cats were waiting for me inside the house, but as had become their habit, they hissed when they saw me and scurried deeper into the house. I went upstairs to wash off whatever lingering scent upset them. I felt disoriented. The adventure had ground to a halt so quickly that it was almost jarring. Just that morning, we'd been looking forward to the spirit medium's arrival, hoping he could give us some information on Helen and praying it wouldn't be bad news. Now, in less than an hour, Lukas was gone again, and Anna had locked herself back in her house. Once again, I was alone with my cats and my cooking.

Following the shower, I peeled the plaster off my finger. I'd changed it several times since cutting the skin, but the marks were finally starting to heal. I held it up to the light. In amongst the dark lines of clotted blood, I thought I saw a sliver of brown. *The splinter's still in there. Damn it.*

My fingers itched to retrieve the needle and have another go at it, but the last thing I needed was to reopen the wound. I resisted the temptation and fixed a new plaster over the marks.

Back in the kitchen, the doll on the windowsill had fallen over once again. I set it upright. Then I went about making a simple dinner. I felt flat, without a purpose, and slouched into the lounge room to eat. One window overlooked the street. The other captured the front part of Marwick House. I alternated gazing between the two of them. Lights came on in different parts of the building, though it was hard to tell which were from Anna. The street was quiet. I watched Penny's house, but she didn't appear in the window.

A low, grumbling growl made me startle. I sat up straighter. The outside world was dark; I must have fallen asleep in the chair. My neck was stiff, so I rotated it to loosen it.

Bell crouched on the chair by the window. She grumbled in the back of her throat as she watched Anna's house. I scowled at her. "Oh, be quiet."

One ear swivelled towards me before returning to the Marwick house. I stood and stretched then froze. A red sports car was parked on the opposite side of the road.

Damn, damn, damn. I wished I hadn't fallen asleep. I crouched and crept closer to the window, keeping myself low so that I wouldn't be seen. The car's windows were tinted, but I caught a hint of movement inside. Raul hadn't yet approached the house, at least. I reached for my phone then swore internally as I remembered I didn't have Anna's number. She'd taken mine but hadn't given hers in return.

I needed to warn her about the car, but I didn't want to walk out where Raul would see me. Instead, I snuck out of the lounge room, keeping low until the walls closed around me and protected me from being seen, then rose and jogged out the back door.

The white picket fence dividing our properties wasn't high. I used a decorative rock to give me some height then threw myself over the fence. I hit Marwick's dry ground, grunted, and rolled to my feet.

Anna had locked her back door. I knocked then called out, trying to make my voice loud enough for Anna to hear without it carrying to the street. "It's Jo! Let me in!"

It took a minute, but then the bolt clattered as Anna unlocked the door. I didn't like standing in the yard and slipped inside as soon as I could. "Sorry, I'm really sorry, but Raul's back."

"Oh." She sounded emotionally dead. I squinted at her, trying to read her face, but she turned away before I could get a good look at her. "Thanks for telling me."

"Something's wrong." I shut the door behind us and turned the light on. "What is it? What happened?"

She still wouldn't face me, so I grabbed her arm and turned her around. In the light, it was easier to see that her eyes were rimmed with red and her cheeks were blotchy. She stared at me a moment, then her face scrunched up as fresh tears started to fall.

"It's okay, it's okay." I pulled her into a hug and patted her back. "I'm sorry for telling you so suddenly. It'll be okay."

She hiccupped, trying to control herself, and took a shuddering breath. "It's the dolls. No one wants them anymore."

"What?"

She pulled out of the hug and wiped her hands across her face. "I uploaded a new batch today. They usually sell out within minutes. But no one's bought them. And they're leaving such horrible comments—"

Anna broke into sobs again. I hunted through the kitchen until I found a box of tissues and pressed some into her hands. "You're okay. This is going to be okay. I'm sure...I'm sure there's just a mistake or something. Do you want me to take a look?"

She hesitated then nodded. "They're all upstairs." ·

I suppressed a shiver at the idea of returning to the blue room and fixed a smile on my face before Anna could see. "All right. Let's see what the problem is."

We climbed the stairs together. A crawling sensation of being watched ran over my back, and I struggled to ignore it. *Don't react. Don't feed the ghost.*

The blue room's door groaned as Anna pushed it open. The desk had been cleared of paints and miniature clothes, and a laptop had been set up beside a row of five dolls. A small digital camera sat on the nearby shelf. I stepped close to the dolls, preparing to praise them, but the words choked off in my throat.

They were horrifying. Like something out of a B-grade horror movie where a doll stalks and murders its family. The lips were pressed into severe lines. The eyes were wide and intent but not warm. They reminded me of wolf eyes. Hungry. Fixated.

One doll had a splatter of red streaks across her arms and face. All she needed was an axe to complete her ensemble.

"What do you think?" Anna whispered. She stood behind me, fingers tangled together in anxious anticipation.

I didn't want to tell her they were a disaster. She was heartbroken enough. But I couldn't believe she didn't see how hideous they were. "Um…why don't you tell me about your inspiration for them?"

"Well, I wanted to try something new. All of my dolls are usually smiling. And I thought, it's not normal for a child to smile all the time. Sometimes they want to look calm and peaceful, you know? So I was thinking of calling these my serene line."

I motioned towards the doll at the end of the line. "And the blood?"

Anna's anxious smile dropped. She looked from the doll back to me as fresh tears ran over her cheeks. "It's paint. She's meant to be an artist. That's why she's wearing a painter's smock."

I didn't know what to say. Anna pressed her palms to her eyes as hiccups built in her chest. "They're not good, are they? People are commenting. They're saying they're ugly and evil and a bad joke. But I really, really tried so hard…"

"I know." I put my arm around her shoulder and carefully led her out of the room. "I know, you tried so hard, and you put so much love into them. But I think this house is affecting you. It's affecting how well the dolls come out. It's not your fault. You haven't done anything wrong."

We stopped at the top of the stairs. Anna leaned on the bannister, staring over the foyer and the windows overlooking the street. She rubbed her nose with the back of her hand. "Is Raul really back?"

"Yeah. I'm sorry. He's parked across the road."

"What am I going to do, Jo?"

I squeezed the arm I held around her shoulders. "It'll be okay. We'll work it out."

"I don't want to be alone tonight."

"Then I'll stay with you."

CHAPTER 20

WE PUT ON A movie and sat wrapped in blankets in Anna's living room. We both studiously avoided mentioning anything to do with ghosts, though I was followed by the horrible, persistent feeling that something hung in the darkest corners of the room, watching us.

Don't acknowledge it. Don't feed it.

The movie's dialogue washed over me. We'd chosen a generic action flick this time, but I struggled to follow its plot. Half of my attention was directed towards the front porch. I couldn't peek through the windows because Raul might see the curtain move, but I was sure he was still out there, watching.

What's his plan? Is he there to intimidate? Is he waiting for Anna to leave her house so that he can grab her?

Anna dozed off near the end of the movie. I repositioned the pillow under her so that she wouldn't get a sore neck, then stretched back in my chair. I wished Lukas hadn't left. A little bit of moral support would have gone a long way.

The clock clicked over to midnight. I was starting to grow sleepy but didn't want to doze off yet. I tried changing my position several times, each rotation contorting into a new, even less comfortable arrangement, to keep myself alert.

The plaster on my finger was itchy. I picked at it absent-mindedly then flinched as a small stab of pain radiated out from the healing cuts. I looked down. Tiny black lines, like stained veins, spread from under the bandage. Horror bloomed inside of me. I traced one of them down; it went as far as my knuckle.

Someone pressed on the piano's keys. The notes held for a moment, then the melody started up, enveloping me, filling my head. I wanted to scream and cry and throw things. But instead, I made myself sit very still. *Don't engage. Don't encourage.*

It was nearly impossible not to, though. The music was unbearable; hot anger threaded through my chest, choking my lungs and my heart, making me feel ready to explode. I pressed my hands over my ears and clenched my teeth together.

A loud bang came from outside, followed by a choked, furious yell. The piano fell silent. I removed my hands from my ears. Anna stirred and sat upright, her eyes huge. "Did you hear that?"

"The music?"

"No, the yell."

I looked towards the windows. "Yeah. D'you think it's..."

Anna scrambled out of the couch and scurried into the foyer. She pulled aside one of the curtains flanking the door and peered through. A horrified cry strangled in her throat, and she hurried to unlock the door.

"What happened? Hey, slow down—"

My friend was already outside. I ran after her, shivering in the freezing night air. One of Anna's trash cans waiting on the curb had been tipped over. Bags of garbage were scattered across the walkway.

Anna stopped beside the bin, her hands gripping her hair, and stared down the road. Without streetlights, very little was visible except for where the moon painted highlights on top of the trees and houses.

I came to a halt at her side and grabbed her arm. "What is it? What's happened?"

"He went through my trash," she moaned. "He found it, and now he knows."

I looked at the garbage scattered across the ground. The bin had a dent in it, as though someone had kicked it over. I swallowed. "Raul did this?"

"Yes, he had to, and he found it." Tears ran over her cheeks. "Why am I so stupid? I shouldn't have thrown it out. I shouldn't—"

"Tell me what's happening. Tell me what he found."

She grabbed my shoulder hard enough to bruise. Raw terror contorted her face. "I'm *pregnant*, Jo. I took a test. It came back positive. I threw it out, but now he's found it. He knows. He'll want the baby—"

"He's not going to get it." I pulled her into a tight hug. She cried on my shoulder, her tears soaking through my shirt and making me shiver. "We'll make sure he doesn't. But...I think you'll need to leave Marwick House. It's too dangerous. Not just because of Raul, but..."

"I know." Her words were so badly muffled I almost couldn't understand them. "I know. I don't want to, but—but—I *know*."

"All right." I glanced about the street, afraid the neighbours were watching us cry over spilt garbage. No one was. All curtains facing Marwick House had been drawn. "Here's what we'll do. We'll go back to my house for tonight. We'll be safer there. And tomorrow, we'll start making plans. We'll find you a new place for you to stay."

She leaned on my shoulder. I kept close to her for both comfort and warmth; I was wearing thin pyjamas, and the asphalt was icy against my bare feet. We turned into my garden. Neither of us cared that Marwick House's front door had been left open. We knew no one would try to go in.

My front door was ajar. *I mustn't have shut it properly.* I pushed the door open and turned on the hallway light and took a relieved breath to be back inside an insulated house. I nodded for Anna to head into the lounge room. "I'll get you something to drink. What do you want?"

"Anything warm."

"Hot chocolate?"

"Sounds good."

As I turned into the kitchen, prickles of uneasiness grew over my arms and shoulders. Something wasn't right. I frowned as I pulled the saucepan out of the drawer and set it on the stovetop. Nothing looked any different. Except…

The doll was missing off the windowsill. I reached for the space it had sat in as the uneasiness grew into visceral fear. My heart thundered. Adrenaline spread through my limbs. My mind raced to catch up to my body, to comprehend the cause of the panic.

A boot squeaked on the tiled floor, and suddenly, I understood. I couldn't have left my front door ajar because I'd leapt over the fence to reach Anna's house. Anna and I weren't alone.

I tightened my grip on the saucepan's handle then swung around, arcing the pan like a bat. At the same time, I screamed, "Anna, run!"

The pan hit Raul's unshaven jaw. The impact was satisfying, but it sent harsh reverberations up my arm. The heavyset man grunted and staggered back, slamming into the fridge. The doll fell from his hand and clattered over the tiles. I didn't wait for him to stabilise. I leapt around the kitchen bench and launched myself into the hallway. "He's here! Get out, get to your house. Lock the door!"

Raul grabbed my arm as I passed him. I fell, slamming into the floor, dropping the saucepan and jarring my whole body. I groaned. He tightened his grip and dragged me back towards him. A line of blood ran from his nose, which was now crooked, and cold fury flashed in his dark eyes.

Then he snarled and keeled back. I looked up; Anna stood behind him, her face sheet white, her mouth in a cold, unforgiving line. Red blood painted her hand from where she'd slashed one of my kitchen knives into Raul's shoulder. He turned towards her, grabbing for her wrist, but she darted out of his reach. I scrambled to my feet. Anna grabbed my hand, and together, we raced down the hallway and burst into the night.

"Get back here," Raul bellowed. His pounding feet beat at my floor. I slammed the front door behind myself, praying it would delay him for at least a few seconds.

The street was almost unnaturally quiet. No lights had come on following our screams. No doors opened. No curtains moved. I suspected we could beat on a door for an hour and not get any response. The rest of the world might as well not have existed.

Anna and I skidded around the end of the picket fence and ran towards Marwick. My own house's front door burst open with a horrific crack of fractured wood.

He bellowed, "Anna! Get back here!"

But we were already through her front door. She slammed it behind us, and together, we scrambled to lock it.

"He'll try to kick the door down," Anna hissed.

I glanced around us. The living room wasn't far away, and I tugged on her sleeve to get her to follow me. I grabbed the end of one of the couches while she took the other side. We dragged it back down the hallway to prop it against the door.

The metal handle jiggled as Raul tried to turn it. Then there was silence for a second, followed by a crashing, pounding noise as he began kicking at the wood. He bellowed Anna's name with each blow. It had become a chant, the meaning of the word lost in the furious screams of "Ah-na, Ah-na, Ah-na!"

Then he fell silent. Anna and I had our shoulders braced against the sofa, holding it against the door. Anna's eyes were round and desperate as she glanced at me.

I licked my lips. "Are the other doors locked? The windows?"

"Not all," she whispered back.

"Go, quickly."

We pushed away from the couch and darted in different directions, racing to lock everything before Raul could reach it. I started in the living room, checking that each of its three windows were secure. As I bolted the third, a hand slammed against the outside of the pane. I sucked in a breath and leapt back. Raul's face, distorted with pure fury, glared in at me. He turned his hand into a fist and punched the glass. The pane exploded. He reached through, seeming not to notice or care that fragments of glass were slashing his arm, and tried to grab at me. I'd already moved out of reach. The pane was too small to crawl through, and the hand retreated.

My head throbbed, and my lungs burned. I pressed a hand to my chest as I scanned the empty window, then forced myself to keep moving. I heard and occasionally saw Anna darting through the rooms opposite. More than ever, she looked like a deer, her eyes huge with terror and her long legs propelling her through the house like springs.

We met at the back door, bolted it together, then hauled the kitchen table in front of it. Anna gasped in shaking breaths as she leaned across the wood. "Did he hurt you?"

"No." My head throbbed from where I'd hit the floor, but I doubted it was serious. "Do you think he could climb the walls to get to an upstairs window?"

She swallowed. "Probably not. Maybe."

"We'll lock them just in case."

Sharp banging on the door made me flinch. Raul had made his way around to the back of the house. The handle jiggled then fell still, and a moment later, Raul called out, his voice softer and coaxing, "Anna, honey, don't be like this."

She shot me a look. We slipped away from the back door and towards the stairs.

Raul's voice floated to us, almost whining. "I want to talk, baby. I miss you. I miss *us*. Why are you being like this? I just want to talk!"

We crept up the stairs. Raul was silent for a moment, then there was a loud *thud* followed by a swear word as he punched the door.

"He's drunk," Anna whispered. "He gets like this when he's had too much."

"Ah-*naaa*." The word was a plaintive whine. "Why are you doing this to me? Do you want me to beg? I miss you, baby. We weren't so bad together, were we?" He paused, then the voice took on a hint of anger. "You *need* me. Stop being so dramatic, and stop embarrassing yourself. Come and unlock the door. *Now*. Before I start getting angry."

We moved through the upstairs rooms one at a time, locking windows. Raul was silent for nearly a minute, then he bellowed in frustration and began kicking the door again. Anna and I ended up in the blue room, surrounded by her dolls, their eyes glowing in the moonlight. We crouched behind her desk and listened as Raul raged and swore and beat against the door so hard, I was afraid it would break.

CHAPTER 21

DAWN BROKE WITHOUT ME sleeping. Anna, emotionally and physically exhausted, had dozed against my shoulder in patches. I was freezing, my limbs shaking and my muscles stiff, but I didn't want to move to get a blanket. The house didn't feel safe.

Raul had yelled for nearly forty minutes before finally falling silent. The quiet frightened me more than the noise. I didn't know where he was, which meant he could be anywhere. But with the sun came fresh courage. I hadn't heard Raul in hours, so I nudged Anna awake. "I think we're okay now."

She pressed her fingers against her eyes and groaned.

"I'm sorry for waking you," I murmured, "but you're going to feel better after a drink and putting on some warmer clothes."

"Did last night really happen, or was that a nightmare?" She looked down at her hands. Dried blood still marked her fingers. "Oh."

"Are you ready to get up?"

Her blue eyes narrowed. "What if he's still here? What if he's just waiting for us to come out?"

"If he is, it won't get any better by putting it off."

She stared at her hand for a beat then sighed. "Yeah. You're right. Let's go."

Walking through the house sent surreal shivers down my spine. Everything seemed too peaceful to follow the night we'd been through, like the unnatural quiet following a tornado. Thin winter sunlight flooded through the windows, making the wooden floors glow and highlighting flurries of dust. For the first time since I'd stepped into Marwick House, I felt as though the building was at rest. The old furniture no longer seemed lonely, but contented. The stairs didn't groan as deeply. Even the lop-sided animal watercolours appeared serene.

We came to a halt in the foyer. No noises came from the house—not even wood settling. I squeezed Anna's arm. "We should search everywhere. And check the doors and windows, too."

"Yes." We split up, like the night before, and explored the lower rooms. I moved carefully, stopping to listen outside every entryway before peering through, just in case. A hint of motion caught my notice inside the music room. I swung towards it, hands raised, but it was just my reflection in the mirror.

"Jo." Anna's voice echoed from the kitchen.

I hurried to find her. She stood by the open back door, staring out into the yard. Her eyes wide, eyebrows raised, lips parted a fraction, she lifted an arm to point towards the old tree in the back corner.

I turned to follow her outstretched arm then tasted the harsh morning air as I reflexively drew a breath. My heart clenched tightly, and my vision turned black for a split second before clearing again.

We'd found Raul. His black hair had been mussed from a night of frantically fighting against the house's shell. Blood ran from the knife wound on his shoulder to drip down his arm and off his fingertips. Light refracted through a couple of remaining glass shards caught in his other hand. His spine was straight, but his head lolled to the side. The rusted metal chain wrapped around his neck held him a foot off the ground.

I gripped Anna's hand. It was cold and sweaty. My pounding heart wouldn't slow. Raul twisted slowly as the wind buffeted him, and for half a second, he was at the perfect angle for his open eyes to meet mine.

I don't know how long we stood there, fixated and horrified by the macabre portrait laid out ahead of us. It took me a long time to find my voice, and when I did, it still cracked. "We need to get him down."

Anna made a faint choking noise in the back of her throat. Sweat dripped down her forehead, despite the crisp morning air.

I took a breath and stepped into the yard. My heart beat so quickly, I was afraid it would explode. The chains groaned against the tree branch as Raul rotated lazily. He almost looked comical with his blue lips slack and the bags under his eyes prominent in the early light. I stopped just shy of him, beside the animal grave, and stared up at his mottled face.

Faint satisfaction washed over me. It seemed right for Raul to be hanging in the back of Anna's house. It was justice—and not just for her, but for him, as well.

I reached towards the chain cinched around his neck. The metal was cold, like his skin. As I touched it, the chain clinked, then Raul collapsed to the ground. I gasped and leapt away from him. His body rolled to a halt at the base of the tree, dirt and fragments of dead grass trapped in his stubble and hair, his eyes staring at me blankly.

I folded my hands behind my neck and tried to calm my racing heart. Part of me expected Raul to start moving again—to stand up, shake himself off, and yell at me for disturbing his rest. But there was no mistaking how dead he was. No living human's skin was that grey.

What are we going to do with him? I looked behind myself. Anna had come up beside me, walking so carefully that I hadn't heard her footsteps. She rested her hand on my arm, her eyes shining with both fear and a small, desperate triumph.

"He can't hurt us anymore," she whispered into my ear. "Helen took care of him. Just like she did with her own husband."

A shiver shook me. I swallowed the thick saliva pooling in my mouth. "We need to get rid of him," I whispered back. "We can't…we can't…"

I lifted my eyes. A woman stared at me: Faye Richmond, Anna's neighbour on her other side. The elderly woman stood by the fence, staring into Anna's yard, her narrow eyes skipping from Raul's body to us. She made eye contact, her mouth tightened a fraction, and she turned and walked away.

No. I backtracked away from Raul. Faye was an irritable woman. She would call the police, and the police would think Anna and I had killed Raul. They had no reason not to. He couldn't have hung himself. Besides, Anna had stabbed him with my knife. He would have left blood trails all around my house and hers. Who *wouldn't* suspect us?

"Stay here." I squeezed Anna's arm and jogged down the side of the house. A bizarre conviction filled me. *If I just explain myself and ask very, very politely, she might not share our secret.*

I ran to my house first. The cats were nowhere to be seen, but Raul's blood still coated my kitchen floor. He'd left handprints on the walls. There was no time to clean them. I grabbed a basket and towel and two of the cakes I'd baked during my cooking frenzy. I bundled them up in the basket and raced back outside.

Faye's house was a modest but impeccably tidy building. She seemed to structure her entire life within rigid guidelines; even the flowers bordering the walkway to her front door had been trimmed to keep them within their designated space.

I knocked on the door. My heart was in my throat, and my sweaty palms left wet patches on the basket's handle. For the first time, it occurred to me that she might not even open the door. She could be cowering inside, the phone pressed to her ear, hiding from me like Anna and I had hidden from Raul.

But the door opened. Faye stood before me, her eyes severe

over her pinched nose and her grey hair immaculately permed. "Can I help you?"

"Yes." I hesitated, waiting for any kind of reaction, perhaps a gasp or a recoil, but Faye only blinked at me. I held out the basket. "I wanted to talk to you about a very important matter."

"Very well, come in. Shoes off, please."

Her house was just as tidy as her person. It made me feel a fraction embarrassed for how dusty some of my own shelves were. Faye took me to what was clearly designated as a guest area, and I placed the basket on the coffee table before taking my seat. She sat opposite, her eyes flicking to the basket, and I had the distinct impression that it was too untidy to be in her house.

I knitted my shaking fingers together. "Mrs. Richmond, I want you to know that Anna and I haven't done anything wrong."

Her severe eyes didn't leave mine. I felt as if I were explaining my poor behaviour to an unkind teacher.

"What you saw—I can explain it. We didn't... I mean—"

She picked a tiny hair off her skirt and flicked it away. "I suppose you're referring to the gentleman in your yard."

I could only nod helplessly. "It's not what it looks like."

"It's none of my business what other people do in their homes, child," she said curtly. No one had called me "child" in a very long time. "Just clean up after yourselves."

I stared at her, not fully trusting what I'd just heard. That was when I noticed her eyes. I'd been so focussed on the severe wrinkles around them as they were narrowed at me that I hadn't noticed how glassy her pupils were. Even though she spoke lucidly, it was as though she'd fallen into a trance.

"We will." I spoke slowly, feeling my way.

"Accidents like this happen," Faye continued brusquely. "I can understand that as well as anyone else. Just clean him up, child, and don't put it off, or it will only get worse."

"That's wise advice. Thank you."

She reached forward and used a fingertip to flick back the cloth covering my basket. "Is that fruit loaf?"

"Yes. To thank you for being a kind neighbour."

She sniffed, but I thought I saw her mouth twitch with a hint of pleasure. "Well, neighbours must look after each other, mustn't they? I don't normally eat such rich food, but I can make an exception. Thank you for visiting. I'm always happy to give advice if you need it."

"I know. And, uh, thank you again, Mrs. Richardson."

She stood, and I knew my audience was over. Faye followed me to the door and shut it with a firm click behind me. I stood on the doorstep for several minutes, trying to understand. Something had changed about our street over the previous weeks. The alteration had been so gradual that I had barely noticed, but now that I searched, proof was everywhere.

Mr. Korver across the road pretended to be watering his plants. He held the hose in a slack hand, the stream falling on the driveway instead of the garden, as he stared into the distance. The water had built up into a small pool around the leaf-clogged gutter. If he noticed me staring at him, he didn't respond.

Penny Crawford's window was empty. Its chair sat in its usual place, framed by the curtains, but I hadn't seen her in it in days.

A car drove past. As it neared the Marwick house, it curved away from the building, its wheels bumping onto the sidewalk. The driver's face remained placid, as though he didn't even realise what he'd just done.

I turned back to Anna's house, my steps sluggish now that I wasn't pushed by urgency. Our street had changed. I decided I liked it. I'd always been a little bit odd, especially so since my mother's death. It was nice to be surrounded by like-minded individuals.

Anna waited in the backyard, where I'd left her. I saw the same glassiness in her eyes as Mrs. Richardson had worn. I went to her side and put my arm around her.

"You were right. The house is protecting us." I kept my voice low, because I knew the subject deserved a reverential tone. "It's looking after us."

"I knew it would." Her voice held a strange lilt, and a smile tugged at her lips. "I knew, as soon as I stepped into it, this would be my home. I would care for it, and it would care for me."

"It's a good home."

"A very good home."

"Should we bury him now?"

"Yes, we'd better."

CHAPTER 22

I DUG THE TIP of my shovel into the dirt, pushed on the handle, and tipped the soil into the growing mound beside us. Flakes of white littered the dark brown. Anna worked beside me, her breathing laboured but her face serene.

We hadn't even needed to discuss where to bury Raul. The answer was obvious. That corner, under the tree, just seemed *right*.

We unearthed our first burial, the owl, early in our dig. Its feathers collapsed off its decaying body. Tiny white worms writhed about as we shifted the body out of the grave. It would need to be returned once Raul was buried; that was a given. Once something was added to that corner grave, it was supposed to stay there.

Anna didn't talk, and I was happy with that arrangement. I needed to do a lot of thinking, but the thoughts that passed through my head were fleeting and vague. Occasionally, I felt a niggling sensation that something wasn't right—that I should be concerned by the things I'd seen that morning—but those feelings always fled as soon as I reached for them.

I dug until my back ached. Hundreds of bones came out of the grave. I didn't bother examining them like I had the first time we'd buried the owl. They were dead, and dead things served no purpose except to be buried.

Anna worked at my side. Perspiration glistened over her face. I thought she shouldn't be exerting herself so much when she was pregnant, but the lazy fogginess washed that idea away within seconds. If Anna was concerned for her unborn child, she didn't let it slow her.

My shovel threw a scoop of dirt out of the grave for the last time. I straightened, knowing that we'd reached the correct depth, at the same moment Anna unbent beside me. The dirt walls came up to our shoulders. We stared at each other for a second. A wild part of me wanted to ask why we were burying a dead man, but the impulse passed unvoiced, and we threw our shovels out of the grave.

The muscles in my shoulders and arms screamed as I leveraged them to get me out of the ground. I tumbled past the mound of fresh dirt, rose to my feet, and turned towards Raul.

A small silver glitter drew my eyes to his back pocket. I reached out and hooked one finger through the metal loop. Out came the keys to his sports car. I turned them over, appreciating them in the light, then threw them behind myself.

Neither Anna nor I wanted to touch Raul. We used our shovels to get under him and roll his stiff form over the edge of the grave. He hit the compacted dirt below with a satisfying *whump*. We smiled at him, admiring the way he'd landed on his stomach, with his neck twisted at an odd angle and one eye peering up at us. Then we began shifting the dirt back into the ground.

It was a slow task, but watching Raul disappear beneath the black dirt and bones was immensely satisfying. I pictured how he would slowly melt away down there, his flesh merging with the dirt and his bones joining those of the animals around him. It was a beautiful image; it made me laugh.

Sweat dripped down my back and over my limbs. It mixed with the dirt coating me, turning it into mud. A little after lunch, Faye Richardson came into her yard to hang out her washing. Her eyes passed over us, and she gave me a curt nod. I nodded back. It was good to have considerate neighbours.

Anna and I didn't stop until the ground had been filled in. We had to beat the soil with the backs of our shovels to compress it. When that stopped being effective, we jumped on it. Eventually, the mound only protruded from the rest of the yard a little. I was satisfied with that and stepped back.

"Good job," I said.

Anna brushed a strand of dirt-matted hair away from her face. "Thanks for helping."

"Of course. Couldn't leave you to do it by yourself." I took a deep breath and let it out slowly. "It's going to rain soon."

"I noticed. Helen must have arranged for the storm. It will wash the blood off the outside of the house."

"There's a hole in your living room window. Make sure you patch it, or you'll get water on your carpet." I tilted my head to the side as I stared at the grave. "I'm going to go home, okay? I want a shower."

"Yeah, me, too. Talk to you later, Jo."

"Bye, Anna."

As I walked across the backyard, I stopped to scoop the car keys off the ground. Then I went around the side of the house and followed the short walk back to my own yard.

Mr. Korver still stood by his garden across the road, his hose pointed towards his feet as the water trickled down the drain. I waved to him. He waved back.

My cats still hadn't returned. I was a little relieved by that; they made such a fuss whenever I visited Marwick House, and I was sure they wouldn't like the way the dirt smelled. I left clumps of it over my hallway and stairs as I climbed them.

The shower heated quickly. Plumes of steam rose around me and fogged the mirror as I peeled off the dirt-caked clothes and dropped them into the bathtub. They would need to be thrown out…but that was something to deal with later.

The hot water felt good on my sore muscles. I washed slowly and had to shampoo my hair twice to remove all of the sediment. When I stepped back out, I felt revitalised. I stood on the bathmat for a moment, dripping but not minding, as I admired my hand. The plaster had come off while I was digging the grave, and I could admire the thousands of black veins that spread from the finger, across my hand and onto my arm. I traced the maze as far as it went; it stopped a few inches past my wrist. I wondered how long it would take to cover me. What would it feel like when it reached my brain? My heart? I laughed, imagining that it would probably tickle, then I went in search of clean clothes.

The light on my phone's message bank flashed as I passed it. I pressed the button and listened to the message as I dressed. Lukas's voice was distorted by the machine but still recognisable.

"Hey, Jo. It's me. I wanted to check that everything was okay. With you...with Anna...with the house... If you need me, I can—"

Irritated, I pressed the button to delete the message. Lukas had no business butting into our lives. We were fine, Anna and Helen and I. We didn't need him messing anything up.

I plaited my hair then returned to the kitchen. Raul's blood had dried on the side of the fridge and the tile floor. I boiled the kettle and found some bleach then resigned my sore muscles to another few hours of work.

The blood came up without too much resistance. It left some light stains on the grouting, but that didn't bother me. I followed the drips down the hall, out the front door, and scrubbed them off my driveway, too. I found Anna's doll, which Raul had taken, partway down the hallway. A drop of blood marred its face. I washed it off with a damp cloth, being careful not to damage the painted features, then sat it back on the windowsill.

By the time I tipped the last bucket of water down the sink, it was nearly dinnertime. I returned downstairs to find my phone ringing. I answered it and set it on speakerphone while I pulled food out of the cupboards.

"Hello?"

"Jo, it's Lukas. Didn't you get my message?"

"I did. Just didn't feel like returning it."

His tone turned frosty. "Seriously? I've been worried. I kept thinking something had happened—"

"Plenty of stuff has happened." I laid pieces of bread on a plate and began spreading peanut butter over them. "Just nothing you need to bother about."

The phone was silent for a few moments, and I hoped he might have actually hung up. Then he said, "Jo, you sound strange. Are you okay?"

"I'm fine."

"Blink twice if you're being held hostage."

I might have laughed at that joke once. But that afternoon, with my muscles sore and my stomach empty, it just annoyed me. "Look, I've got a lot of work to do. I'll call you if there's anything I think you can help with. But I'm not expecting there will be."

"Jo, seriously, you're starting to worry—"

I ended the call. I couldn't stand hearing his self-righteous voice any longer. He was just as bad as his mother; they wanted to gloat from a distance, mock me, and laugh about how much better they were than weird, stupid Jo. Well, I wouldn't give them any more opportunities. If Lukas tried to visit, I would lock my door.

The sandwich didn't taste right. I'd nearly finished it by the time I realised I'd spread tomato sauce over it instead of strawberry jam. It would take too much effort to make a new one, so I finished it and threw the plate into the dishwasher.

There was one more thing I needed to do that evening. I plucked Raul's keys off the kitchen bench, donned my jacket, stuffed a towel into my pocket, and stepped outside.

Twilight had fallen, which would help mask my presence. I walked up our street, peering into driveways and connecting roads. Almost no one was outside. Those who were didn't look at me. It was peaceful.

I found Raul's red sports car parked a block away under a thick oak tree. I unlocked it and slid inside. The plush leather seat tried to embrace me. The sensation was repulsive, but I repressed my shudder and closed the door before starting the engine.

The drive to the nearest beach took more than an hour. It was a scenic route. Except for the distasteful feel of the leather, I enjoyed the ride. I parked in a lot overlooking the beach.

The storm wasn't far from breaking. Spits of water hit my face as I stepped out of the car, and the salty wind whipped my hair around my face. A handful of other vehicles were scattered around, their families braving the weather for a final afternoon at the beach before winter made it intolerable, but no one was nearby. I pulled the towel out of my pocket and wiped across the steering wheel, the leather seats, and both internal and external doors. I took a lot of care to clean any surface I'd touched, though I didn't think it would matter much even if they found my fingerprints. I wasn't a suspect, and I'd never been convicted for a crime, so I wasn't in any database to match. Even if they thought Anna might be responsible for Raul's disappearance, her prints wouldn't match any from the car. No one would think to question her neighbour. Why would they?

I left the keys in the ignition and the door open. With luck, someone would steal the car, further masking the trail. If not, the police might come to the conclusion that Raul had drowned himself in the ocean. His girlfriend had left him just weeks before; it wasn't impossible to think he might be depressed.

I tucked the towel back into my pocket then bowed my head against wind and thick, icy raindrops. It would be a long walk back home. But I didn't mind; it would give me time to fill my head with thoughts of nothing.

CHAPTER 23

THE STORM BEGAN IN earnest shortly after I'd started the walk home. I tightened my jacket around myself and ducked my head, but it didn't take long for the rain to saturate me.

I must have walked for hours, but a comfortable haze had descended over me. By the time I raised my head and saw I was in my own street, the rain had settled into a drizzle. I was surprised to get home so soon, even though it must have been after midnight.

Bed had never felt so good. I didn't even bother drying myself—I just threw off the wet clothes and crawled under the blankets. A dreamless sleep came immediately. Not even the lights switching on in Marwick House disturbed me.

The rain had cleared by the time I woke the following morning, though residue still dripped from the roof and the trees. I rose, rubbed the sleep out of my eyes, and went about the tasks still to be completed that day.

My clothes needed to be thrown out. Not just the ones I'd worn while digging the grave, but the rain-soaked ones, as well. I bundled them into garbage bags and carried them to the nearby park. A family played on the still-wet swings, but they didn't glance at me as I forced my bags into one of the large bins. It was just another layer to mask the fact that Raul had ever been in Anna's street.

I felt lighter on the way home. I had no doubt Anna would have been doing her own cleaning. The neighbours wouldn't say a word. If Raul's disappearance was ever traced back to Marwick House, the evidence would be scant. I grinned as I re-entered my home.

The following days passed quickly. I watched the news for any mention of Raul, but his name only appeared once, in a police request for information. Reading between the lines, I sensed he wasn't a high-priority case for them. A missing adult man wouldn't carry the same weight as a lost child.

I didn't see much of Anna. We kept to our own homes, much like the neighbours around us. Occasionally, we waved to each other over the fence. But our closeness had ended with Raul's burial. And I think we were both grateful for it.

My cats were all missing. Scared off by the house, I guessed. Part of my mind worried about them, but it was easy to quieten it. I'd loved them once—adored them, even—but lately, I rarely felt any kind of emotion. The cats were just another possession. Maybe they would turn up one day. If they didn't, I wouldn't lose sleep over them.

I stopped baking, too. Most days were spent sitting in my living room, staring at a wall or at the TV, its channel set to static. I found it easier to soothe my mind like that. The stillness was only disturbed when I needed to water my garden, hang out laundry, or prepare food. I did my tasks with a machine-like precision, starting them and finishing them at the same time each day. Lukas didn't try to call again. The world was peaceful.

One afternoon, as I made my way from the kitchen to the lounge room, I caught sight of Anna through the window. She'd pulled her curtains back and stood behind the glass, staring blankly at me. I raised a hand. She didn't respond. I continued to my favourite chair, turned on the TV to absorb its static, and relaxed.

Two hours later, I was due to water the plants. I rose and saw Anna still standing in the window. She had bags under her eyes, and her hair was limp and had lost its sheen. Again, I raised my hand in greeting. She didn't respond. She wasn't even blinking.

Something shook loose inside of me. *This is wrong. What we're doing—whatever's happening—it's wrong.*

My feet were unsteady as I passed the full washing machine and stumbled into my backyard. I blinked in the sun. Though the day was cool but fair, it didn't stop the overwhelming unease blooming through me. I looked to my right. The grave was visible over the fence; it had nearly completely sunk down to ground level, thanks to the rain. Soon it would be covered by the tree leaves, then even I wouldn't remember its significance.

"No." I spoke the word out loud, feeling as though it would

have more power that way instead of rattling around in my mind. "Something's wrong. Something's wrong. No. Stop it."

I turned and strode back into my house. My fingers dug into my hair, scratching at my scalp as I paced. The black threads were spreading farther up my arm; they'd passed my elbow that morning.

"Wrong, wrong, wrong." I grabbed the phone off my living room table. There was no one in my life I could call except for Lukas, so I dialled his number. The phone rang a single time. I hung up. Some part of my mind was telling me I couldn't call him—that I would be putting both Anna and myself in danger if I did. I tapped the phone against my chin as I paced, trying to clear my head enough to see what needed to be done.

I came to a halt facing the window that overlooked Anna's house. Across the fence and behind a second sheet of glass stood my friend, unmoving, unresponsive. She'd been there for hours.

Understanding dawned over me. *That's what the problem is. The house was never this active before. It never started affecting other people in the street before. It never affected* me *like this before. It's because of Anna. No...not Anna...but the thing inside of her. The baby. That's what's caused all of this wrongness.*

I couldn't believe I hadn't seen it before. The spirit medium, Henry, had talked about Helen having a secret she needed to protect from her husband. She must have been pregnant when she leapt from her window. She'd decided it was kinder to lose her own life, and the life of her child, rather than watch them both suffer at the hands of her husband.

And that was why she'd latched on to Anna: the young woman was nearly a mirror of Helen's situation. A secret child. A violent partner. A desperate need to hide—to escape—to be safe.

Helen had gone insane in her desperation to protect Marwick's new occupant. And it was tearing everyone and everything apart.

I pressed my hand to the window, willing Anna to respond to me. Her blank stare landed somewhere past my shoulder. I swallowed, and the frustration, fear, and anger that had welled inside me coalesced into an understanding of what I needed to do.

The doll on the kitchen window stared at me with its dead eyes. I couldn't stand being watched by it any longer; I turned it around to face the glass. Then I pulled out my favourite bowl, my beloved and dented mixing spoon, and turned on the oven.

I hadn't been shopping recently, which meant I was low on some of my staple ingredients. I ended up pulling together enough for a sponge cake with jam and mock cream. I sifted the dry ingredients, enjoying the weight of the neglected sieve and appreciating how fine the flour looked as it cascaded into the bowl. I added the sugar then finally opened the highest cabinet in the back of my kitchen to retrieve the porcelain jar.

It had been my mother's. She'd kept it in the cupboard beside her bed. I'd seen it there several times while cleaning, but it was so unremarkable that I hadn't given it much thought. It wasn't until after her death and the coroner's report came out that I'd realised what it was: iodine.

On top of the diabetes, my mother had been poisoning

herself in tiny increments. I still don't fully understand why. Was it a way of increasing the severity of her symptoms? Giving herself more excuses for calling the doctor? Or had she done it to punish me, in the same way she would wet the bed if I was late bringing her dinner?

In the days following her death, I'd replayed a thousand scenarios through my mind, each designed to hurt me more than the last. I pictured my mother taking a pinch of the iodine any time I forgot to bring her drinks on time or whenever I refused to give her sweets or when I forced her to take her medicine. She hadn't said a word about the jar, but each time I displeased her, it would have pushed her a little closer to death. And that was the beauty of the punishment: I only felt its sting when it was too late to apologise and too late to right the wrongs.

The day my mother finally died had been especially challenging for me. I'd had a migraine—one of the bad ones that made me nauseous and blurred my vision—and my mother had been demanding. She never liked it when I was sick—it took the spotlight off her. So she'd made me run a dozen minor errands for her: rearranging the blankets around the stumps of what used to be her legs, fetching a fresh glass of water because she didn't like the taste of what she had, and retrieving an extra pillow, which was thrown on the floor an hour later.

I'd reached my limit by mid-afternoon. The migraine was blindingly painful, and I couldn't stand the sound of her voice for another minute. So I went outside to the shady garden seat where I could lie down and drape a cloth over my eyes to block out the light. It helped. I fell asleep and didn't wake for hours. By the time I roused, it was night, and my mother was dead.

The memories swam through me, alternately stinging and punching at my insides, as I popped the lid off the jar and stared at the white powder inside for a long, sad moment.

I don't believe my mother had intended to die that night. She wasn't depressed and had shown no inclination for death before then. She probably hadn't realised the dose was enough to kill her. But she took it then wrote one of the cruellest notes she could manage.

The words surged through me, threatening to drown me: *I blame you for the way I've ended up. In a fairer world, I would have had a child that loved me the way they should.*

That note was memorised. I'd read it countless times in the days following my mother's death.

When the coroner's report came out, highlighting iodine poisoning, it naturally sparked a police investigation. I was ultimately cleared of blame, but by that time, I'd fully internalised the idea that my mother was dead because of me.

I'd managed to hide her porcelain jar. Once the funeral was over and the police investigation finalised, I took it out of hiding, opened it up, and baked two tablespoons of the white powder into my favourite spice cake. When it came out of the oven, I cut myself a slice, poured fresh cream into the bowl, and sat down to eat it.

For three hours, I stared at the cake. I was weak, frightened of what awaited me after death. What tortures did hell hold for children who killed their parents? Eventually, I threw out the slice.

You still have the rest of the cake, I told myself. *It will keep for a few days. You can eat it any time.*

Days went by. I don't remember much of that time, except that Lukas came to stay. He was the only member of my family who seemed to care more about me than what was in my mother's will. He'd offered to help clear out the house. I don't know if he realised how close to the edge I was, but his voice had held that careful, gentle concern that frustrated me so much.

But he'd done me some good—not just to shake me out of my fog, but by finding the documents hidden at the back of the filing cabinet. Apparently, my father's will had left half of everything he owned to my mother, and half to me. My mother had concealed my portion—from jealousy, possibly, or out of a fear that I would leave if I had financial independence. She'd always told me she'd received everything he had. But the papers showed I'd inherited a not-insubstantial sum. It was enough to live on for five or six years. And it let me buy my own house. Somewhere far away from the town I'd grown up in. Somewhere, coincidentally, beside a haunted building.

I'd brought the iodine with me, not with the intention of using it, but to have it there just in case. As weeks turned to months, I thought of it less and less often. Some days, I almost fully forgot it was there.

I dipped a measuring spoon into the powder, scooped up a heap of the white granules, and scattered them over the flour.

It was tasteless and odourless. Anyone who consumed it wouldn't know until the convulsions started. I mixed four tablespoons of the iodine into the dry ingredients before adding the milk and eggs. Four tablespoons would be plenty for someone eating a small slice. The mixture combined beautifully. I resisted the temptation to dip my finger in then poured the batter into a pan.

Washing up while waiting for the cake to cook gave me time to clear the anger out of my head. I joined my doll in looking through the window towards Marwick House. I felt better now that I had a purpose. It was the only way to fix Anna, even if it meant I would never see her again. The house would go back to being quiet. Dormant. Perhaps it would stay empty for another eight months before a new family moved in.

CHAPTER 24

THE CAKE SMELT GOOD. I decorated it with icing sugar before wrapping it in a cloth and leaving the house. Anna still stood at the window when I passed it, but she answered the door on the third knock.

Her face was grey and gaunt, and her eyelids red. She looked sick. Pity twisted inside of me, and I held out the cake. "I brought you a treat."

"Thank you." The voice didn't sound like hers. It was too flat. Too deep. She turned and walked towards the kitchen. I followed, feeling as though I'd joined a two-person procession. We went through our usual tasks with smooth efficiency: boiling the kettle, pouring water into the cups, slicing the cake, setting out plates. Anna served me a piece, though I had no intention of eating it.

I felt the need to make some kind of conversation. "Things have been quiet."

"Yes." Her blue eyes seemed darker than normal. "Very."

We sat at the table, one on each side, and Anna picked up her fork. I watched her cut a corner off the cake's slice.

"How are the dolls?"

"They haven't sold." She lifted the cake to her lips. Slipped it inside. Chewed. Swallowed. "So I won't make any more."

"That's a shame."

She didn't ask why I wasn't eating my cake. I watched her cut off another forkful. Something shifted inside my mind. *This is wrong.*

My eyes were blurred, I realised. How long had they been like that? Why hadn't I noticed before? I shook my head, and dullness sloughed away from me. When I blinked my eyes open, a thousand shades saturated the room. I was shocked to realise I hadn't been perceiving colour over the last few days.

I looked at Anna. She looked back, her face dull, her eyes glassy. The implications of what was happening rushed over me, and I startled upright, knocking my chair over.

Anna placed the second cube into her mouth. "What is it, Jo?"

"No. No, no, no, no—" A curtain had been lifted from my eyes. I stared about myself, horrified, unbelieving of what I'd done. Anna returned her fork to her cake like a machine, neatly cutting off a third cube. I lunged forward and smacked it out of her hand.

She stared at me, but her eyes didn't hold shock, only very mild surprise. There was no life behind the heavy lids. Terror ripped through me. I'd poisoned my friend. She'd eaten two bites—was that enough to kill her? The baby? I grabbed her shoulders and shook her. "You've got to throw up. Please, Anna, I'm sorry—"

Those emotionless eyes stared back at me. The voice, which sounded less and less like my friend with every word, released a soft, emotionless laugh. "You're so strange, Jo. It's a nice cake. I would like some more."

"No, Anna, listen to me—it's been poisoned. Think about your baby. You don't want to hurt your baby, do you?"

Her lips twitched into a smile. The voice was now unrecognisable. "Perhaps it's for the best."

I slapped her as hard as I could. Her head snapped to the side, and her eyes widened. She raised a hand to her cheek, where a splotch of pink appeared on the pale skin, and the awful glassy sheen vanished from her eyes. It was replaced with fury. "Don't touch me!"

"Listen, Anna—"

She threw herself at me. We grappled, and I fell to the ground. The impact winded me. She pushed me down and pressed one knee onto my chest to keep me there. Her whole face was turning bright red from anger as her scrabbling hands found my neck.

I tried to speak, but her grip tightened and squeezed my throat shut. I thrashed, trying to throw her off, but my energy was already low, and she had the height advantage. Her thumbs dug into my trachea.

Then she blinked, and the anger was replaced by shock. She scrambled away from me. Her hands were still held out ahead of herself, but they shook. "Oh-oh no. Jo, I—"

I fought to regain my breath and propped myself up against a wall. "You didn't mean to. I know."

"Jo." Tears welled in her eyes and spilt over her cheeks. "What's happening, Jo?"

"It's Helen. I think she wants one…or both of us…dead." I rubbed my sleeve over my forehead to remove the sweat. "You need to throw up. I poisoned the cake. Be quick, before any's absorbed."

Horror drew over her face, then she scrambled to her feet and dashed to the sink. I listened to the sound of running water and retching, and the terror squeezing my chest relaxed.

I looked down at my hands. They were both flesh-coloured. The awful discolouration that had been growing up my arm had vanished. I hoped it had only been an illusion.

Oxygen was returning to my limbs. I dragged myself to my feet and moved around the kitchen table. Anna leaned over the running sink. She looked ghastly. One hand held her hair out of the way, and tears rolled down her cheeks and dripped off her nose freely.

"Is it all out?"

She nodded.

"I'm so, so, so sorry." I pressed a hand to Anna's shoulder. She reached up her free hand and squeezed mine.

"You said Helen was doing this. But why? I trusted her—I thought she was looking out for me—"

"I think she was, in her own strange way." I reached up to get a glass from the cupboard and filled it with running water. I handed it to Anna, and she downed it. "She was pregnant. I'm almost certain. That was the secret Henry mentioned, the child she didn't want her husband to discover. She threw herself out of the window because she believed it would be safer for them to be dead."

"And she thought the same for me." Anna's eyes narrowed. I watched them closely in case the glassiness returned, but they appeared clear. She wiped her hand across her mouth. "She wanted me dead. Like her."

"So you'd never be apart. So she could look after you forever." I turned off the tap then leaned my back against the bench. "It's irrational. Especially when she already took care of Raul."

Anna groaned and bent low over the sink again. "I forgot that happened. It feels like a dream. Did we really bury—"

"She was influencing us. A lot. Just like she influenced everyone else in our street. I haven't seen any of our neighbours in days." I ran my hands through my hair, which was tangled and overdue for a wash. "We need to leave. We're not safe as long as we're in this house...or even this street."

"Yes." She pushed away from the sink. Her hair hung in her face, sticking to the sweat, and she tried to brush it aside as she glanced around the room. "I'll just get my dolls—"

"No. There's no time." Now that I'd realised what we needed to do, a desperate urgency propelled me. I grabbed Anna's arm and pulled her through the kitchen. "She'll try to pull us back under her trance. We need to get as far away from her as we can, as quickly as we can. We'll—we'll stay with my aunt and Lukas.

They'll let us move in for a couple of days while we figure out what to do."

Anna's lips quivered. She swallowed and glanced towards the stairs as we passed them. "Can't I pack a few things? Everything I own is here. My whole world."

That sounds reasonable. It will only take a minute to fill a travel case. She can gather her clothes while I pack the dolls…

I blinked. The thoughts tried to cling to my mind like cobwebs, but I brushed them away. I understood what was happening. "No. It's Helen making you think you want to pack. She's trying to stall you, because every second you spend in her house, she tightens her grip a fraction." I bent closer, staring into Anna's eyes, willing her to absorb some of my conviction. "We'll go right now. In a few days, we can come back and collect your things."

She fixed her lips together and nodded. I'd gotten through to her. I wondered if she realised the promise to come back was a lie. I knew in my soul we would never see Marwick House again. We would be like the last family—the ones I'd watched run to their car, crying, wearing only their pyjamas. They had never returned. And like them, Anna's property would be absorbed into the building to be used and admired by the next soul who underestimated the house and Helen's control over it. I wondered what they would think about the blue room with its shelves of smile-less, dead-eyed dolls.

We ran to the front door, and I grabbed the handle with both hands. I was ready to get outside, to taste clean air again, and clear my head of the layers of fog Helen had wrapped it in. I was ready to see my family. I was ready to be free.

The door handle wouldn't turn.

CHAPTER 25

"WHAT—" I RATTLED THE handle. It was frozen. I felt around the locks, bolting and unbolting them again, but none of them were engaged. The door wouldn't open. "Anna? Do you know why it won't turn?"

"No." She turned to scan the foyer as she folded her arms across her chest. "Let's use the back door."

We held hands as we jogged through the house. The house's dignified silence felt magnified as we ran into the kitchen and towards the back door. The handle rattled when I twisted it, but then stuck. I groaned. "No, come on, let us out. We're not playing your games anymore."

Anna stepped into my place and struggled with the door. She beat her fist against it then kicked it before finally slumping against the wood. Colour had drained from her face. "She's locked us inside."

I pressed my hands to the sides of my head. I couldn't believe it. We were so close to getting away—just a thin block of wood divided us from safety.

"We'll find a way out." I turned towards the house and raised my voice. "You can't keep us here!"

A door slammed upstairs. We both flinched.

"Come on. We'll get through a window." The pane above the kitchen bench was large enough to squeeze through. I leaned over the sink and tried to open it, but the clasp had frozen shut. I strained until my hands ached before sliding back. "We'll need to break it."

Anna had already pulled down two of the heavy cast-iron pots from the stovetop. She handed one to me then heaved her own at the glass. A deep, angry clang shook in my ears as the metal struck, and bounced off, the glass.

"No way," I muttered, swinging my own pot at the window. Reverberations ran down my arms as the pot bounced back. The window remained flawless.

Anna didn't speak, but her face tightened with anger. She beat her pot against the glass again and again, filling the kitchen with the awful discordant clangs, then slumped back, breathing heavily. "There are other windows. Bigger windows."

"Okay." I already knew it would be wasted energy—but I couldn't give up without trying. We raced through the house, first beating on the tall dining room windows, then the square panes in the laundry, and finally facing the large latticed windows in the living room.

One of the panes was already broken. Raul had punched through it on the night he'd died. Anna had taped a square of cardboard over the hole, but I ripped it back and crouched down. Cool, fresh air blew in. I used the pot's handle to apply pressure to one of the glass fragments poking out from the wooden sash bars crisscrossing the window. I leaned my whole weight against it, but the glass didn't pop out. It didn't even crack.

The hole was big enough to pass an arm through, but no wider. I dropped the pot as I stepped back. "I can't believe this. She's sealed us inside." I thought of the great owl we'd buried. It had snapped its neck on an upstairs window, but the glass hadn't shattered. I wondered if Helen had always had such control over the house, to protect it and strengthen it.

Anna bent close to the broken pane and cupped her hands around her mouth. "Help! Help us, please! Help!"

I pressed my forehead against the glass and scanned the street. The chair in Penny's window stayed empty. Mr. Korver was no longer in his garden, but his hose lay on the lawn, forgotten.

"Help!" Anna screamed, slamming her open palm against the window. "We need help!"

They're not going to answer. People always used to avoid Marwick House, but now it's worse than ever. We need to contact someone who's outside of Helen's reach.

"Where's your phone?" I shook Anna's shoulder. "We'll call Lukas."

She dashed into the hallway and grabbed the handset off the table. "Here."

I had Lukas's number memorised. I dialled it and held the phone to my ear. All I heard was static. I swore and redialled the number. Then I smacked the phone and checked its batteries. I couldn't see any reason for it not to work.

Anna chewed on the corner of her thumb as she watched me. Hope was fading out of her face. I tried the number a final time and held the phone up to my ear.

There was something in the static. I frowned and pressed the phone closer. It sounded like breathing.

"What is it?" Anna whispered.

I held up a hand to ask for silence. The static crackled. And inside, muffled by the distortion but unmistakable, a woman sighed.

Chills raced up my arms. I slammed the phone back into its cradle. Anna's expression was tight. I rubbed my sweating palms on my pants. "We'll get out of here. I just need to…to think for a bit. Yes. We'll sit down and talk it over. I'm sure we'll figure something out if we approach it rationally."

"Jo…"

I patted her arm and turned towards the living room. "We'll be okay. Come and sit with me."

"Jo, no." She grabbed my sleeve and tugged me back. I felt a swell of frustration. Didn't she see I was trying to help?

"Let go, Anna."

She gripped my shoulders and shook me. Hard. "Jo! Snap out of it!"

The cobwebs had been accumulating over my mind without

me even noticing. I blinked as they melted away. The world had begun to blur, but as the cobwebs dissolved, it swam back into focus. "Uh…"

"Wake up!" Tears ran down her face. "We don't need to sit. If we sit, she'll trap us in our minds again, and we'll never get out. We need to keep moving."

My heart lurched. I rubbed shaking hands over my arms. "I'm sorry. I wasn't thinking—"

"I know." She sniffed and rubbed her hand over her nose. "It's so easy to fall back in. You just need to stop thinking for half a minute, and she'll dig her claws into you."

"That means we can't leave each other alone. Not even for a moment." I squeezed her hand. "We've got to stay alert and look out for each other. Yeah?"

"Yeah."

"All right." I turned to face the house. My mind felt sluggish, but I forced it to think through our situation. "We can't get out through the doors or the windows. And no one outside is going to come looking for us. What else can we do?"

"We still have the herbs and salt from the cleansing." Anna shot me a frightened glance. "Henry said not to try it again, but…"

"But I don't think he expected us to become trapped like this," I agreed. "It's worth a shot. Where is it?"

"In the storage cupboard. This way."

I followed her towards the music room. As we pushed the door open, the curtains shifted. I tried not to stare at them as we went to the vast cabinet in the back of the room.

A soft, barely-audible twang came from the piano. The dark wood shone in the lights. A small puff of dust swirled off its top.

Anna wrenched open the cupboard doors. The space was empty except for dust and the abandoned cleansing instruments: the sprig of sage, box of matches, and plastic container of salt. We shared a look, simultaneously dreading trying to use the items and clinging to hope.

"What did you want to do?" Anna whispered.

I remembered she hadn't like the way the sage smelt when it burned. "I'll do the herbs."

"Then I'll take the salt."

We turned back to face the room. Henry had started the process by opening the house's windows, but they wouldn't budge. I hoped that wouldn't stop the cleansing from working. I took up the sage bunch and the box of matches. Anna collected the container of salt and opened the top. We stared at each other for a second. Anna cleared her throat. "It would be faster to split up—"

"No. We keep together."

She nodded. I struck a match and touched it to the bundle of dried herbs. They caught, and the smoke began to rise as I held them ahead of myself. Anna began spreading salt across the floor. Henry seemed to have a pattern he scattered it in, but I couldn't remember how he'd done it. I hoped our inexperience wouldn't disadvantage us.

"Throw some on the piano," I suggested.

Anna collected a handful of salt and tossed it over the instrument. As the grains touched the wood, an awful, ear-splitting clang burst through the room, as though someone had pounded on the keys. We both flinched away from it. The jangled notes hung in the air for what felt like forever, but I managed a smile as they began to fade. "I think it's working."

"I think you're right." She was breathing heavily but laughed. "Let's try some on a door."

The kitchen was closest. We hurried into it. I passed the burning sage around the door's edges as Anna threw a handful of salt across it. Then I tried the handle.

It was still locked.

"Okay." I tried to control my disappointment. "It's not helping—yet. But it must be weakening her, right? If we keep going through the house, we might be able to loosen her hold."

Anna nodded. She was already scattering the salt around the benches and window.

We worked through the house methodically, spreading sage and salt everywhere we could reach. The house stayed quiet, as though it had expended its energy on the piano. The sage's leaves were blackening and withering faster than I would have liked. As we passed through the living room, I nudged Anna's arm. "This sage is burning quickly. I don't have much left. How's your salt?"

"Low." She shook the container.

"How about we go upstairs? Helen was trapped in that blue room for who-knows-how-long, and died by throwing herself from the window. If her energy is going to be concentrated anywhere, it will be there."

"Right." She squeezed her hands around the salt container.

I led the way up the stairs. As I passed, I waved the sage around the watercolour portraits. I don't think it was my imagination that the puppies and kittens and foals seemed to shiver away from the smoke.

The upstairs hallway was dark. I tried the light switch, but none of the lamps turned on. I shot Anna a questioning look over my shoulder. She nodded that I should continue on.

As I passed the first room—the master bedroom—the door groaned closed. I swung towards it. With a click, the latch caught in the doorframe. I shifted closer to the opposite wall as we circled past. The next door along the hall creaked as we drew near. I watched as it slowly, lazily turned on its hinges before finally clicking closed. The bathroom was next. As I passed it, the tap squeaked, followed by the rush of pouring water.

"She's trying to distract us," Anna said. "Keep going."

I fixed my attention on the door at the end of the hall. There was a flash of motion as the grey curtains shifted in a breeze that didn't exist. Its door stayed open even while the ones on either side of me shuddered closed. I took a deep breath, my heart thundering, and held the burning sage ahead of myself.

CHAPTER 26

WE STOPPED ON THE blue room's threshold. Something felt different about the space. The mental cobwebs were building up over my mind again, blurring my eyes and slowing my reactions. I glanced at the hand holding the sage; the black veins spread down my arm, going nearly all the way to my shoulder. I blinked. They were gone again.

"Stay alert," I hissed. "She's trying to pull us back into her trance."

I stepped into the room and was slapped by a sense of surrealism. The shelves still stood against the walls, their blank-faced dolls staring down at the doorway. But the desk below the window was gone. In its place lay a cot. Pink lace had been painstakingly sewn around it, and a rattle rested on its edge, ready to be given to the infant inside.

A small, gurgling cry came from the crib. Enthralled, I stepped closer. There was no child inside. Instead, one of Anna's dolls lay amongst the soft sheets and pink cushions.

The doll bore a striking resemblance to its creator. Long, mousy hair spread out from its head. Its eyes were large and clear blue. The arms stretched out, and at first glance, they seemed to ask for a hug. But then I saw the blood trickling from the back of the doll's head. Its plastic cranium had broken open from the fall that had flung its limbs wide. Its lips were parted in a tiny, surprised smile. The shining eyes held no life.

I choked out a cry as I stumbled back from the image. Anna was at my side in an instant. She threw a handful of salt into the crib, and sick, icy shivers ran up my limbs. I blinked, and the cot was gone. Only the desk remained in its place, the malformed, unsmiling dolls glaring up at me.

"You're okay," Anna whispered. "It was just a trick. Put it out of your mind."

She turned towards the window, and I followed her gaze. Night had fallen and obscured the yard, but I thought I saw something large move in the back corner.

"Raul's hanging there again." Anna's voice was raw. "We buried him, but...but he's—"

"Back," I finished. "Don't look at it. It's another illusion."

"Spread some more sage." She took a quick breath and pressed my arm as she moved past me. "You were right. Helen's strength is concentrated here."

I raised the bunch of herbs. The smoke spread through the room, hanging about the corners and blurring the walls. Anna scattered fistfuls of salt across the dolls, the desk, and the windowpane.

"Get that corner, too." I nodded towards the place where holes had been drilled into the wall. When I looked closely, I could see a rusty outline from the bracket Helen had once been chained to.

Anna tipped salt across the wall and the ground. Tiny plumes of black smoke rose from the floor, as if the salt were burning the wood. My herbs were burnt down to stubs, so I threw the bunch into the corner. "I'm out."

"Me, too." Anna shook the empty salt container. "Do you think it was enough?"

"I don't know. Let's see." I went to the window and grabbed the frame. It rattled and shifted up an inch. Cool air floated through the gap. I strained, alternately yanking it up and down, trying to shake it loose. I stepped back, my breathing laboured.

"It could just be jammed." Anna stepped up and tried the window herself. It still stuck. "Jammed from a natural cause, I mean. Come on, let's try the front door."

"All right." I reached out and gave the frame a final yank as Anna stepped into the hallway. It only moved up an inch before freezing again. I sighed and turned to leave the room.

Something crouched in the corner where I'd thrown my smouldering sage. I froze, my heart thundering, as Helen raised her head to glare at me. Her tousled hair hung like curtains around her face, and her faded steel-blue dress was grimy. Metal clinked as she shifted, and I saw a long chain running from a collar around her throat to the wall.

"Anna?" My voice was a squeak.

Anna was already halfway down the hallway, but she stopped and turned at my voice.

With a snarl, Helen's lips parted. One hand moved forward to cover her belly. She was ringed by the salt, and the sage's smoke drifted past her face, but she didn't seem to notice or care.

Anna was coming back up the hallway. "Jo, what is it?"

"She's here." I raised a hand to halt Anna. "Don't come in."

Helen shifted a fraction, her grey eye sparkling behind the hair. It was heavily ringed by shadows. I bent forward and dropped my voice into the gentlest whisper I could manage through my fear. "Helen, I'm sorry about what happened to you. It was awful. Unforgivable. But you don't need to be afraid any longer. Anna and I—we're here to help you."

"I don't need your help." The voice was gravelly and cracked, words passing through a throat rarely used. Helen shifted forward. The chains clinked. She wore no shoes, and her nails had grown lengthy. I wondered how long she'd been kept up here.

"Helen, we just want to leave. Let us out, and you can have the house to yourself."

"I don't...want...the house." She shifted her weight from one side to the other, swaying, her long hair falling forward to obscure the eyes again. She bared her teeth in a cold smile. "I want *her*."

A bony hand rose to point to the doorway. Anna stood in the opening, eyes huge and terrified.

I guessed Helen's intent a second before she moved. "*Run!*" I yelled, dashing towards the door at the same instant as Helen lunged after us. She was fast. Long fingernails scored across the back of my shoulder as Anna and I raced for the stairs. I couldn't breathe. Helen was gaining. Another second, and her bone-thin fingers would grasp my arm—

The chains clanged as they were pulled taut. Helen released a gasping cry, and her pounding footsteps ceased.

Anna and I hit the end of the hallway. We turned to look behind ourselves. Helen had vanished. The door to the blue room stood open. Inside, the grey curtains shifted in the breeze.

"You okay?" Anna asked, squeezing my arm. I couldn't speak, so I nodded instead.

The lights went out with a hissing whine. Anna and I clutched each other close. Night had surrounded us, and without the downstairs lamps to share their glow, the house was pitch black.

We waited, crouched at the top of the stairs, for the lights to come back on. They didn't. Anna took a shaking, gulping breath. I could feel her trembling. "We'll try the door. If it d-doesn't work, there are torches d-downstairs. In the kitchen."

"Okay." I couldn't take my eyes off the place where the blue room would be. Everything else in the house was dark except for one small, glinting circle. It looked like an eye peering out from behind curtains of hair. I nudged Anna towards the stairs. "Don't let go of me. I don't want to lose you in this dark."

We inched down the stairs. Having to move without my eyes made me sick to my stomach. I used my foot to trace out the edge of each step before climbing down it. I knew the stairs were all the same height, but in the dark, it didn't feel like they were.

Progress was laboriously slow.

A chain link clicked, and Anna flinched. I squeezed her hand. *Keep moving.*

My feet touched the uncarpeted foyer. I began breathing a little easier and released my grip on the bannister. Anna rose out of her crouch and led me towards the front door. I listened to her fingers scrabble over the wood then touch the handle. The metal rattled. She groaned deep in her throat.

"It's not opening?"

"No."

A deep note pinged through the still air. I knew what was coming and squeezed my blind eyes closed. The melody started.

"We need the torches." Anna's voice held an undercurrent of bitter resignation. "This way."

We turned, and I let her lead me deeper into the house. I ran my free hand along the walls as we felt our way through the maze of rooms. I stubbed my toe against an unseen piece of furniture and gasped.

"All right?" Anna asked.

"Yeah."

Both of our hands were clammy, but we didn't let go of each other.

The floor changed from wood to tile, and I knew we'd entered the kitchen. I waited for Anna to feel along the wall and count the drawers. The melody, slow and full of ponderous intent, swam around my head. A drawer clattered as it was pulled open, then Anna rummaged through the contents and inhaled as she found something.

Sudden light made me blink. The torch's beam sent weird shadows playing over my friend's features. The sallow-skinned woman stood behind her, one hand curled around her shoulder, leaning so close that their hair tangled together.

Then Helen was gone again.

CHAPTER 27

I GRASPED THE SENSATION that made me want to scream and squeezed it back down into the pit of my stomach. Anna saw the look on my face, and her triumphant smile faded. "What is it?"

"Helen. She's not trapped upstairs."

Anna glanced over her shoulder, almost as though she'd felt the presence that had lingered there. Then she closed her eyes. "I'm so sorry, Jo."

"What for?"

"Dragging you into this mess." She opened her eyes. Tears shone in them. She turned her torch towards the drawer and began rummaging. "She wants *me*. You shouldn't have gotten tangled in this."

"Not your fault." I gave her a thin smile. "If anyone's to blame, it's me and my ridiculous curiosity. I just couldn't stay away."

"Here." She turned on a new torch and passed it to me. "These were here when I moved in, so the batteries are going to be old. I don't know how long they'll last, but they're something."

"I'll save mine, just in case." I turned it off and tucked it into my back pocket. Then, using Anna's torchlight to see the way, I went to the back door and tried its handle. It stuck, too. I ground my teeth. "All right. The salt and the sage didn't work. What's the next step? Is there any way out of this building that we're overlooking?"

Anna chewed on her lip. "Just the two doors as far as I know. And the windows."

"Is there an attic? A basement with an exit leading outside?"

"Ah—yes! I've seen a basement exit down by the side of the house. One of those wooden trapdoors."

"Good, we'll try that." The cobwebs were starting to gather over me again, so I shook them away. "Remember, stay alert. Keep moving. It's easier to stay alert that way."

"Wait, Jo. I don't know how to get into the basement."

I stared at her, and she gave a helpless shrug. "I never found its door."

"There's got to be a way. We'll search for it. C'mon."

I'd never imagined I would become as familiar with Marwick as I had. Anna and I looped through the house, staying close to each other as we opened every door we passed. We looked in cupboards, in wardrobes, and behind curtains. As we searched through more and more of the house, my hope began to wane. The piano's incessant melody bore into my mind, making me feel sluggish and miserable. *Maybe the basement is only accessible from outside. Maybe we're wasting our time.*

"Found it!" Anna cried, and the maudlin dropped away from me. We were back in the foyer. She'd opened the cupboard under the stairs. I jogged to catch up with her.

"Look," she said, pushing a row of umbrellas out of the way. "I thought it was just a cupboard, but there's another door inside it."

"It's a good hiding spot," I said, running my hand over the thin line marking the door's edge. "Let's go."

We threw the umbrellas into the foyer. The door was locked and didn't have a handle, so I backed up and kicked it. The wood fractured on the second impact, and the third sent it banging open. Damp, musty air blew out of the gap and stuck in my throat. Anna turned her light into the hole.

A set of stone stairs led down into the pitch dark. When I shifted into the cupboard, heavy echoes rose up from the basement.

I licked my lips. The area was giving me a bad feeling. I didn't want to take the stairs—but there was no alternative. We had to keep moving.

"Want me to go first?" Anna asked.

"No, that's okay. I'm just…" Again, the cobwebs snagged over me. *Maybe we should wait until morning. It will be safer then…* I shook my head to clear it. "No, I'm ready."

I stepped into the dark. A metal handrail ran along the wall. I reached out to hold it, but the metal was badly rusted and had a slimy, tacky sheen. Pulling my hand back, I grimaced.

The air was colder down in the basement. It held a lot of

trapped moisture that condensed over my skin. Anna alternately pointed the torch at our feet and panned it across the basement's assortment of clutter. Judging by the dust and cobwebs clinging to everything, I knew it hadn't been visited in a very long time. Possibly not since the Marwicks had perished.

I counted the steps. *Twenty.* They'd been carved unevenly, almost as though the basement had been added as an afterthought. The steps levelled out into a flagstone-plated floor. Thick wooden support beams rose out of the ground to brace the higher rooms. They were spaced unevenly around the basement, and long black shadows flitted across the wall as Anna's torch passed over them. They reminded me of thick prison bars. I shuddered.

"Where's the trapdoor?" Anna muttered. She sent her circle of light jumping over the boxes and shelves littering the area. "The stairs faced the kitchen, which means…" She turned, and her torch landed on a square of wood set high in the wall. "Ah-ha."

"Good spotting." I wove through the clutter to reach the door. It was above my head, and there weren't any stairs leading to it. "Damn. Look for something we can stand on."

Anna rooted through a stack of rusted gardening implements. "There's a wheelbarrow here. It's metal."

"Good." We each grabbed one end of it and dragged it under the trapdoor. It made a horrific screech as it scraped across the stones. I wiped a hand over my forehead then stepped onto the wheelbarrow. "Keep your torch on the wood."

The barrow was sturdy but not steady. It wobbled as I stood on it, and I pinwheeled my arms to stay upright then grabbed the stone wall to keep myself steady. Anna took a few paces back so that her light would cover a greater area. I felt along the thin crack between the small doors, but there was no bolt on this side. I pushed and felt resistance.

"They're locked from the outside."

Anna muttered something furious.

"Hang on." I pushed against the wood again, testing my stability and the trapdoor's sturdiness. "If the lock was installed at the same time as everything else in this basement, it'll probably be rusty. I might be able to break it open."

"Okay. Be careful."

The wheelbarrow shifted on the uneven floor as I applied more pressure to the wood. I adjusted my stance on it then pushed harder. I heard some kind of metal groan. That was a good sign. I pushed harder.

Upstairs, the music was building up to a crescendo. I'd never heard the song all the way through before, and I wished I didn't have to then. The doors bowed slightly as the lock bent. I tasted hope. Whatever Helen had done to the upstairs doors, she hadn't done to this one.

The torchlight turned away from me, leaving me in darkness. I didn't dare move my stance while the wheelbarrow was so unsteady. "Anna?"

"Just a moment. There's something here." I heard a scrape of what sounded like cardboard being rubbed together, then a flutter of paper.

"Anna, don't let her distract you."

"I'm not. I mean, she's not. But look at this."

My stomach turned cold. I resumed pushing on the wood. "We're so close. I just need a bit more leverage, and I can get this open—"

"These are psychiatric admission papers. They're for Helen."

I relaxed the pressure on the door and turned. Anna bent over a large filing box. A sticker on the side read Armidale Sanatorium. Anna held up a page for me to see. It was some kind of form. I couldn't read the writing in the poor light, but the photograph paperclipped to the sheet showed a familiar face. Dark, resentful eyes looked out from under a mess of black hair.

The wheelbarrow creaked as I warily climbed down from it. "She was admitted?"

"Yeah, in 1944."

I moved closer to read over Anna's shoulders. Her hands were shaking, making the paper tremble in turn.

"Psychiatric wards weren't kind to women back then." A flush of colour spread over Anna's pale skin. "Raul would... He would sometimes try to scare me by telling me stories about what happened to women in them. He'd make it sound like it still happened. Like he could put me in one if I stepped out of line."

I put an arm around her. "He was a jerk."

"Hah, understatement." She scrubbed at her eyes. "Anyway, back then, a husband basically had control over whether his wife went into one or not. All he had to do was tell the doctor she was acting irrationally, and she'd be put away. She couldn't try to argue that she was sane because that's exactly what a crazy person would try to tell you."

I frowned. "That doesn't make sense, though. Helen didn't die in a sanatorium. She died at home."

"What if…" Anna ran her finger down the patient notes. Phrases jumped out at me such as *paranoia, mood swings, violent tendencies, hysteria.* "What if the opposite happened? What if she was actually, really mentally unwell, but her husband didn't want to leave her in an institute? What if he knew she'd be mistreated there, so he looked after her at home, instead?"

"Huh." I remembered the chain in the upstairs bedroom. If Anna's theory was true, it wouldn't have been a way to trap Helen, but a way to keep her safe. "Penny across the road said Helen would disappear for days or weeks at a time, and when she came back, she'd be covered with bruises. What if her husband was hiding her away whenever she relapsed, and the injuries were self-inflicted?"

"That would make sense. If she was paranoid—maybe some kind of schizophrenia or multiple personality disorder—she could be fine one day and then violently dangerous the next."

The song ended with a heavy, crashing clang, like someone had slammed their hands on the piano keys.

Anna's eyes flitted over the paper. "And what if, during one of her psychotic episodes, she pulled her chain out of the wall, believed her husband was trying to hurt not just herself but also her secret child, and threw herself out of the window?"

My mind was spinning. "What if she never had a child?" I

glanced towards the ceiling. Long-forgotten cobwebs clustered along the support beams. "Penny never mentioned anything about an unborn baby. But one would have been found if there'd been an autopsy…and there must have been an autopsy because it was such a sensational crime story. Besides, Helen and Ray had been married for nearly seven years before her death. What if she desperately wanted to have a baby but wasn't able to?"

"If we're right, that means Ray killed himself from grief, not guilt." Anna frowned at me. "I almost don't want to believe it… but it fits together perfectly."

A floorboard above us groaned. Small streams of dust rained from between the support beams. I bumped Anna's shoulder. "Whatever happened back then, Helen is dangerous. We need to get out. I've almost got the trapdoor open."

"Okay. I'll put these back." Anna began shuffling the papers back into the box. I thought I saw unshed tears shining in her eyes. "I don't feel right leaving them out in the open."

I climbed back up onto the wheelbarrow and pressed my hands to the doors. Like before, the barrow wobbled, nearly dislodging me. I reset my stance and began straining. I felt the metal give way another fraction of an inch.

The torchlight moved away from the door. I heard the scrape of cardboard as Anna fit the box back onto the shelf. Then, with a click, the light turned out.

CHAPTER 28

"ANNA?" I PAUSED TO glance over my shoulder. "Did the battery run out?"

I didn't get a reply. Fear dried my mouth. I licked at my lips to wet them again. "Anna, please talk to me. Are you still there?"

A soft sigh came from deeper in the room. I let go of my hold on the door and felt for my own torch in my back pocket. *Stupid.* I'd dropped my guard. Putting the box away had been another one of Helen's stalling tactics, and I realised what I'd first taken for unshed tears must have been the foggy veil building over Anna's eyes. The papers had distracted her just long enough for Helen to hook her.

"Anna, wake up! Don't let her take control again!"

I found my torch and fumbled for the switch. The light clicked on. I couldn't see Anna, which meant she had to be hiding behind one of the shelves or support beams.

I shouldn't have taken my eyes off her. She's more vulnerable. She's been closer to Helen and under the fog for longer. It would be easier for her to relapse.

"Anna?" I stepped forward and panned my light across the space. Dust particles drifted through my torchlight. I thought I heard a sound behind me and swivelled. "Think about your baby, Anna. You need to keep it safe. You need to keep it away from Helen. She's not your friend—she only wants your baby."

There was another noise that might have been Anna, or it might have been a rat. I turned but couldn't see anything except the stretching shadows, clusters of boxes, and chaotically spaced wooden beams. "Please, Anna, don't do this to me. We're so close to getting out. Please."

The door at the top of the stairs groaned. I shone my torch towards it, but a wall blocked my view past the first four stairs. I smothered a moan, tightened my grip on the torch, and stepped towards the stairs.

The piano was silent, which was somehow worse. All I could hear were my ragged breaths and pounding heart echoed back to me. It made me feel truly alone.

The uneven stairs made me feel disoriented. The cold, damp air stuck in my lungs and collected over my skin. I found the door at the top of the stairs had been pushed nearly closed. We'd left it open when we'd come into the basement—Anna had definitely come that way.

Cold sweat trickled down my back. I was painfully aware of

the passing seconds. Every additional beat gave Helen more time to cocoon Anna in the heavy, foggy cobwebs.

I stepped into the foyer. The area was perfectly still. No light came through the windows. My torch's beam only picked out small patches of furniture at a time, making them look distorted and unnatural. "Anna?"

I thought I heard a sigh behind me, but when I turned, the space was empty. The animal watercolours on the wall watched me with their lopsided, malformed eyes. The icy air continued to flow out of the basement and sent shivers running up and down my back.

Where is she? I stepped towards the music room. Movement shimmered inside, but when I entered, all I found were the curtains drifting in the still air. My light shone on the piano keys, still coated with dust, then glinted off the golden mirror frame. I turned towards it. A sallow face stared out at me.

"Let Anna go. She's not yours."

Helen's cracked lips parted into a cruel smile. She took a step back and vanished. Hot anger boiled in the pit of my stomach. I grabbed the piano seat and hurled it at the mirror. It hit hard, and the glass exploded into a hundred pieces.

Keep calm. I was shaking. I squeezed my hands around the torch to still them. Without Anna around to watch my behaviour, I had to be hyper-conscious of every action and thought. It would be too easy to be sucked back into the fugue. *Find Anna. Snap her out of it. You've done it once. You can do it again.*

A thought hit me, and I turned towards the kitchen. Helen

wanted Anna dead. I'd left the poisoned cake on the table. If Anna had returned to it, I would never forgive myself.

Shadows leapt about me as I moved from the music room to the back section of the house. A hundred points of light glittered in the kitchen as my torch moved over the pots, tiles, and metal appliances. When I didn't focus on them, they looked like eyes.

The cake still stood on the bench. A partially eaten slice rested on Anna's plate. It didn't seem to have been disturbed since we'd sat down together. *Thank goodness.*

Something else had changed, though. Anna had used a knife to cut the cake then left the implement on the table. But it was missing. I licked my lips and looked behind myself. Had she taken it in self-defence? To hurt herself? Or to attack?

She's still in the house. Somewhere. But Helen's in control. Where would she lead her?

The answer was so obvious that I couldn't believe I hadn't recognised it before: the blue room. The thought of climbing the stairs filled me with nausea. I didn't want to return to the insane woman's den or see her crouched in the room's corner, her black, beady eyes glaring up at me. But I had to. I dreaded to think of what she'd do to Anna if I didn't.

I returned to the foyer. My torch seemed to be growing weaker. Its beam passed over the same furniture, but it didn't illuminate them as well as before. I could no longer see details, only outlines.

The stairs loomed above me, and pounding dread filled my head as I stared at them. I didn't want to climb up. Didn't want to hear the chains again. Didn't want to see the faceless dolls.

Someone sighed. I swivelled towards the noise. Anna stood behind me, her loose hair a mess around her face. Her pallid skin was dotted with perspiration, but her face appeared serene. I met her heavy-lidded eyes and saw the awful glazed sheen I'd been dreading.

"Anna, wake up." I reached towards her, preparing to shake her, and ready to slap her if it came to that. She didn't shift away. Instead, she brought her hand up. I saw the shine of silver and tried to twist aside too late.

The knife slashed along my side. Blinding pain spread from just below my ribs, and I screamed as I collapsed away from Anna, clutching the wound. Hot blood ran between my fingers.

A cold smile twisted Anna's face as she stared down at me. Her foggy eyes glittered, and she exhaled a single, marvelling "ha," as though surprised by my reaction. Then she dropped the knife and turned away.

The blade clattered to the floor at my feet. I tried to squirm away from it. A click followed by a low creak and a gust of wind made me look over my shoulder.

The front door drifted open. I was being let go.

"Anna?"

Instead of answering my call, she began to climb the stairs. Her movements were sluggish, almost robotic, but her head tilted upwards, turned towards where the blue room lurked out of sight.

"Anna!" I screamed the word as loudly as my lungs could manage. She didn't even flinch. I looked over my shoulder again at the door; the street was only twenty paces away. I would be safe once I reached it. I could call an ambulance, and the ambulance would take me a long way from Marwick House. I'd never have to see it again.

But I knew I'd also never see Anna again. Except, perhaps, to identify her body.

She was halfway up the stairs. I pulled my hand away from the gash on my side. It was long but not deep. That didn't stop it from hurting like hell, though. I struggled to tug my jacket off and pressed it to the cut then tied the sleeves around my waist, cinching them as tight as I could stand so that I'd have my hands free. I rolled to my knees and used the bannister to drag myself to my feet.

I'd left the hallway phone on the table beside the stairs. I snatched it up and dialled the emergency helpline. They always took too long to answer calls to Marwick House—but too long was better than nothing. I pressed the phone to my ear. All I heard was static.

Anna had disappeared around the top of the stairs. All of my strength was draining through the cut, but I ignored the burn the best I could and used the bannisters to pull myself up the stairs.

The distorted watercolours watched my progress, their black dabs of irises rotating to follow me. I wasn't imagining it this time.

"Anna!"

The stairs groaned. Just as I had during my first day at Marwick, I felt half afraid that the wooden boards would collapse and plunge me through the floor.

I reached the landing just as the door at the end of the hall groaned closed. I could hear the rattling chains. Interspersed with them was the awful lullaby, hummed by a familiar voice. My legs didn't want to carry my weight. I forced them to, staggering down the hall, blood running from under the makeshift compress and trickling down my leg. I tried dialling the emergency helpline again. Once more, static answered me. The lullaby came through the phone, too, hummed by a second voice but eerily, and perfectly, in tune with Anna's song.

The door was cracked open just wide enough to give me a glimpse inside the room. The window was fully open. The panes had been removed, creating a tall slot in the side of the house. Grey curtains rolled in the force of a gale. The sun hadn't yet risen, but nautical dawn spread a pale, ethereal light across the horizon.

I pushed open the door. Two women moved towards the window. The taller one, black haired and wild eyed, wasn't solid. Her form was more like a whisper—or a shadow—barely visible but still intangible. She stepped through the window to stand on the outside sill.

The second form was solid and familiar. Anna lifted one foot to step on the desk then extended the other through the window. She stood on the same ledge as Helen. Their bodies overlapped, Helen's blending into Anna's like a hologram.

"Anna! *Stop!*" I moved forward, my hand outstretched to grab her.

Anna's movements were perfect replicas of Helen's, only a

second delayed. The women stood on the ledge for a second, then Helen turned to face the room, followed by Anna. They reached their hands out wide, appearing to offer a hug. The wind buffeted them, thrashing their hair about their faces and whipping the curtains out. Then Helen keeled backwards.

"*No!*" I shrieked and dove forward. Anna tipped back, a perfect mimic of the black-haired woman. Her blue eyes met mine, and a hint of recognition flashed through the haze. Her lips lifted into a soft smile. But the awareness came too late. She was already falling.

CHAPTER 29

I REACHED FOR ANNA, throwing all of my strength into a lunge to grab her. My fingertips grazed the loose edge of her cardigan. Then she was gone, dropping away from me, disappearing into the dark abyss below.

My knees hit the desk, and I collapsed against it. I squeezed my eyes closed in sick horror as I waited to hear the crack of her skull breaking open.

There was a heavy *thud*…followed by a gasp.

I blinked my eyes open. The inhalation hadn't come from Anna—but from a man. Hope cut through my pain. I scrambled onto the desk, forgetting about the cut on my side, and leaned my head and shoulders through the window.

Anna lay below. No blood stained the rocky ground. Her head hadn't broken. And she wasn't alone. Her small form was curled in Lukas's arms.

"Hey!" I yelled.

Lukas lifted his head. His face was sheet-white and twisted in pain, but he gave me a thin smile when he saw me.

Something rocked the house. My first thought was that we'd been struck by an earthquake. I scrambled off the desk and crouched on the floor as tremors moved through the building, shaking the walls and sending plaster dust pouring over me. Then the sensation passed as suddenly as it had started, and I pulled in a hacking, coughing breath.

The house felt different somehow. A shadow had been lifted away from it.

I'd dropped the phone on the floor when I'd reached for Anna. I picked it up. This time, when I dialled the emergency helpline, I was greeted by a woman instead of static. I could have cried.

Ambulances and police always took too long to arrive at Marwick House. I wanted to curl into a ball on the blue room's carpet while I waited for them, but the need to be close to my friends outweighed it. I took a moment to fortify my mind then limped along the hall, down the stairs, through the open front door, and along the side of the house.

"Hey." Lukas sat where I'd last seen him, his too-long legs stretched out at an awkward angle and with Anna held in his arms. He nodded in greeting as I rounded the side of the house. "You're hurt."

"I'll live. What about you?"

"Fractured ribs, maybe. She's heavier than she looks. But it could have been worse."

I crumpled to my knees beside him. Anna wasn't moving. Her face was slack, and her body limp. I reached out to touch her arm.

"She's got a pulse," Lukas said. I noticed he was holding her very carefully as he tried not to move her neck.

"What happened?" I sat back beside him and pressed my hands to the jacket. It was sticky with blood.

"That's what I was going to ask you."

"No, I mean, how come you're here?"

"You called me, remember?" His voice was thin with pain, but he managed a smile. "You hung up before I could get to the phone and then wouldn't answer when I called you back. So I figured something had gone screwy. I got here, you weren't home, Anna wouldn't answer when I knocked, and the door was locked. I came around the back to see if I could get in that way. Saw Anna in the window." He shifted his shoulder and flinched. "Figured I may as well get in the way of her fall."

"Hah." I leaned my head against my knee and briefly told him what had happened. He only looked moderately dubious.

"So…assuming all of this is real and you weren't hallucinating…"

"It is, and I wasn't."

"I'll verify that later. But if that's true, are we at any risk here? We're on Marwick ground."

"True." I glanced up at the house. The lichen and vines still coated its stone, but they didn't seem to hold the sinister portent that they usually did. "But I think Helen's gone. I think we completed her loop."

"Huh?"

"Remember what Henry said? Ghosts have loops. Motions they repeat. If you can find a way to break them—to ruin the loop—the ghost disappears."

I lifted a hand to the window then let it flop back into my lap. "Helen's loop was her suicide. She wanted Anna to repeat it, so that she could have Anna—and Anna's baby—for herself. But you broke it. You caught her, just like Helen should have been caught all of those years ago. Boom. Unfinished business finished."

"Boom," he echoed then coughed. Blood appeared on his lips.

The sunrise broke in earnest, and the first rays of golden light hit Marwick House's roof. I turned towards the street, thinking I heard sirens in the distance. *About time.*

CHAPTER 30

Three months later

DUSTY LOUNGED IN HER seat below the window. She rolled onto
her back to expose her belly and pink paws. One eye peeked open
as I neared her, then lazily drifted closed again. I gave her belly
a scratch. She was getting fat. I couldn't help myself. I'd been
giving my cats a constant stream of treats to make up for the
stress I'd put them through with Marwick House.

"Be good," I told her.

She kneaded the air with her front paws as a deep, rumbling
purr echoed from her chest.

I snagged my jacket off its hook on the way out. Even though it was
a bright day, the early-spring air was chilly. I jogged down my front
drive, turned left, then turned left again to enter Marwick's property.

Anna had only been working on the garden for a month, but

the change was dramatic. The grass was starting to regain its colour in patches. Flowers and bushes were taking root along the fence. She'd planted a tree, and although it was only small, I knew it would have a great impact on how the place looked once it had grown a bit. It also had the double bonus of obscuring Penny's view a little. I didn't need to turn to know she was watching me from her window seat.

The front door had been left open, so I rapped on the wood as I entered. "Hello! Just me!"

"Out the back!" Anna called.

The house's air felt still and cool. I followed the familiar path, past the curving staircase I'd once hated and the music room that had tormented me, through the kitchen, and into the backyard. Anna had set up a patio table and chairs. A platter of finger foods and a pitcher of juice weighed down the tablecloth. Lukas was already sitting at her side. I shouldn't have been surprised. He practically lived at Marwick House lately.

Anna stood to give me a hug. She seemed so much happier than before. I sometimes wondered how long she'd been under Helen's thrall—perhaps the first threads had been planted as early as her first week in the house. She smiled and laughed a lot more following the leap from the blue room.

The final tally from that night had run to: one broken rib, two fractures, and a punctured lung for Lukas, as well as a broken leg and a serious concussion for Anna. I escaped with my stab wound, which needed eight stitches and a blood transfusion. We had all spent a couple of days in hospital.

"Sit down, have a drink." Anna ushered me into a chair. "Lukas was just telling me about the new script he's writing."

"Oh, he was, huh? Let me guess: he's finally accepted your fate as a director of haunted house documentaries."

Lukas scratched at his stubble. "No, actually. It's a film about the search for bigfoot." I sent him a confused stare, and he winked. "A *mental* search for a *metaphorical* bigfoot."

"Oh, good, pretentious garbage. For a moment, I was worried you were actually going to make something good."

He laughed. I snuck a glance at Anna's hand. No ring yet, but I didn't think it would take much longer. Not when they were so clearly enthralled with each other. They'd set their chairs as close as they could and even then leaned towards each other. Lukas smiled more often, too, and his barbs were a little less caustic than normal. Anna's presence seemed to be gradually filing down the rough edges.

Anna poured me a drink then resumed her place at Lukas's side. As he rambled about his new project, my eyes drifted to the tree at the back of the yard. While Helen had been haunting Marwick, it was the only plant that had managed to survive. It had started shedding its leaves, and the bark was turning black. It wouldn't survive much longer.

I couldn't stop my eyes from dropping to the patch of dirt below. Rainfall was steadily levelling the raised ground, and grass was covering the bare dirt. Neither Anna nor I ever mentioned what was buried below. We both pretended we didn't remember it, though I certainly did, and I was sure she did, as well. It was our secret—Anna's, Helen's, and mine—and we would never breathe a word to anyone.

"Jo?" Lukas flicked my arm to bring me back to the conversation. "Stop spacing out. You're not an astronaut."

"Sorry, what?"

"Anna was saying she's going to make you work twice as hard after lunch. She's going to be an absolute tyrant."

"I never said that!" Anna squeaked. "I just meant that we have a lot of work today! Eight dolls to mail and two new custom orders!"

I grinned and turned my back to the grave. "I'm looking forward to it. I've been practicing my miniature hand-stitching." I mimed the motion in the air. I wasn't artistic enough to paint the faces, but as it turned out, I'm pretty good at sewing miniature clothes.

"Good. I want to get as many dolls made as possible before this little lady throws my world into chaos." Anna patted her belly, where the bump had started to show. "Do you think, if I beg really hard, Lukas will stay to take the mail to the post office?"

I laughed. "Oh, I think you'll have to beg him to leave."

As Lukas refilled Anna's cup, I let my attention wander. Marwick House creaked behind me, but the sound didn't carry the menace it once had. The building was harmless without its dead guardian. It now stood as an elaborate monument to the blood that had been shed under its shadow, and as a reminder that I had, for four brief years, lived next to a haunted house.

ABOUT THE AUTHOR

Darcy Coates is the *USA Today* bestselling author of *Hunted*, *The Haunting of Ashburn House*, *Craven Manor*, and more than a dozen horror and suspense titles.

She lives on the Central Coast of Australia with her family, cats, and a garden full of herbs and vegetables.

Darcy loves forests, especially old-growth forests where the trees dwarf anyone who steps between them. Wherever she lives, she tries to have a mountain range close by.